# Anxiety

Editor: Danielle Lobban

Volume 422

First published by Independence Educational Publishers

The Studio, High Green

Great Shelford

Cambridge CB22 5EG

England

© Independence 2023

**Copyright**

This book is sold subject to the condition that it shall not,
by way of trade or otherwise, be lent, resold, hired out or otherwise
circulated in any form of binding or cover other than that in which it
is published without the publisher's prior consent.

**Photocopy licence**

The material in this book is protected by copyright. However, the
purchaser is free to make multiple copies of particular articles for instructional
purposes for immediate use within the purchasing institution.
Making copies of the entire book is not permitted.

ISBN-13: 978 1 86168 882 8

**Printed in Great Britain**

Zenith Print Group

# Acknowledgements

The publisher is grateful for permission to reproduce the material in this book. While every care has been taken to trace and acknowledge copyright, the publisher tenders its apology for any accidental infringement or where copyright has proved untraceable. The publisher would be pleased to come to a suitable arrangement in any such case with the rightful owner.

The material reproduced in **issues** books is provided as an educational resource only. The views, opinions and information contained within reprinted material in **issues** books do not necessarily represent those of Independence Educational Publishers and its employees.

### Images

Cover image courtesy of iStock. All other images courtesy of Freepik, Pixabay and Unsplash.

### Additional acknowledgements

With thanks to the Independence team: Shelley Baldry, Tracy Biram, Klaudia Sommer and Jackie Staines.

Danielle Lobban

Cambridge, May 2023

# Contents

## Chapter 1: Anxiety Overview

| | |
|---|---|
| 'Anxiety' named as children's Word of the Year for 2021 | 1 |
| What causes anxiety? | 2 |
| Anxiety, fear and panic | 3 |
| From jubbity to mubble fubbles, anxiety is well catered for in the historical dictionary | 4 |
| Anxiety in autistic children – why rates are so high | 5 |
| Anxiety statistics 2023 | 6 |
| Young lives under pressure as global crises hit mental health and well-being – report | 8 |
| Why anxiety can be good for you – even if it feels terrible | 10 |
| Depression, anxiety and heart disease risk all linked to single brain region | 13 |

## Chapter 2: Anxiety Triggers

| | |
|---|---|
| Covid-19 pandemic triggers 25% increase in prevalence of anxiety and depression worldwide | 15 |
| Young people around the world report high levels of climate anxiety | 17 |
| Eco-anxiety is harming young peoples's mental health – but it doesn't have to | 19 |
| Stress, anxiety and hopelessness over personal finances widespread across UK – new mental health survey | 21 |
| What's driving the female anxiety epidemic? | 22 |
| Phone call anxiety: why so many of us have it, and how to get over it | 23 |
| Why the root of your anxiety might not be your mind | 24 |

## Chapter 3: Managing Anxiety

| | |
|---|---|
| Treatment - generalised anxiety disorder in adults | 26 |
| Tips to look after your mental health during scary world events | 29 |
| 4 relaxation techniques to combat stress and anxiety | 31 |
| Group course can be standard treatment for anxiety and depression, trial finds | 32 |
| Young people to be prescribed surfing and dancing by NHS to help anxiety | 34 |
| A personal reflection: the drugs do work – taking SSRIs for panic disorder | 36 |
| How therapy has helped me begin to tackle anxiety and overthinking | 38 |
| Three ways to tackle the 'Sunday scaries', the anxiety and dread many people feel at the end of the weekend | 40 |
| How to use the 333 rule for anxiety | 41 |

| | |
|---|---|
| Further Reading/Useful Websites | 42 |
| Glossary | 43 |
| Index | 44 |

# Introduction

Anxiety is Volume 422 in the **issues** series. The aim of the series is to offer current, diverse information about important issues in our world, from a UK perspective.

## About Anxiety

According to the Oxford University Press, 'anxiety' was children's word of the year in 2021. Covid 19, climate change & the cost-of-living crisis have undoubtedly contributed to the sharp rise in the number of people of all ages seeking help because of anxiety in the last couple of years. This book looks at different anxiety disorders, the causes, the triggers and various methods to cope with them.

## Our sources

Titles in the **issues** series are designed to function as educational resource books, providing a balanced overview of a specific subject.

The information in our books is comprised of facts, articles and opinions from many different sources, including:

- Newspaper reports and opinion pieces
- Website factsheets
- Magazine and journal articles
- Statistics and surveys
- Government reports
- Literature from special interest groups.

## A note on critical evaluation

Because the information reprinted here is from a number of different sources, readers should bear in mind the origin of the text and whether the source is likely to have a particular bias when presenting information (or when conducting their research). It is hoped that, as you read about the many aspects of the issues explored in this book, you will critically evaluate the information presented.

It is important that you decide whether you are being presented with facts or opinions. Does the writer give a biased or unbiased report? If an opinion is being expressed, do you agree with the writer? Is there potential bias to the 'facts' or statistics behind an article?

## Activities

Throughout this book, you will find a selection of assignments and activities designed to help you engage with the articles you have been reading and to explore your own opinions. Some tasks will take longer than others and there is a mixture of design, writing and research-based activities that you can complete alone or in a group.

## Further research

At the end of each article we have listed its source and a website that you can visit if you would like to conduct your own research. Please remember to critically evaluate any sources that you consult and consider whether the information you are viewing is accurate and unbiased.

## Issues Online

The **issues** series of books is complemented by our online resource, issuesonline.co.uk

On the Issues Online website you will find a wealth of information, covering over 70 topics, to support the PSHE and RSE curriculum.

## Why Issues Online?

Researching a topic? Issues Online is the best place to start for...

### Librarians

Issues Online is an essential tool for librarians: feel confident you are signposting safe, reliable, user-friendly online resources to students and teaching staff alike. We provide multi-user concurrent access, so no waiting around for another student to finish with a resource. Issues Online also provides FREE downloadable posters for your shelf/wall/table displays.

### Teachers

Issues Online is an ideal resource for lesson planning, inspiring lively debate in class and setting lessons and homework tasks.

Our accessible, engaging content helps deepen students' knowledge, promotes critical thinking and develops independent learning skills.

Issues Online saves precious preparation time. We wade through the wealth of material on the internet to filter the best quality, most relevant and up-to-date information you need to start exploring a topic.

Our carefully selected, balanced content presents an overview and insight into each topic from a variety of sources and viewpoints.

### Students

Issues Online is designed to support your studies in a broad range of topics, particularly social issues relevant to young people today.

Thousands of articles, statistics and infographs instantly available to help you with research and assignments.

With 24/7 access using the powerful Algolia search system, you can find relevant information quickly, easily and safely anytime from your laptop, tablet or smartphone, in class or at home.

Visit issuesonline.co.uk to find out more!

# Chapter 1: Anxiety Overview

## 'Anxiety' named as children's Word of the Year for 2021

Expert says word is 'concerning' but 'not surprising'

By Saman Javed

Anxiety was children's word of the year in 2021, according to research by lexicographers at Oxford University Press (OUP).

Prompted by the impact of the Covid-19 pandemic, last year's annual vocabulary research focused on wellbeing.

Approximately 8,000 school pupils – ranging from year three to year nine – were asked to choose the top words they would use when discussing their mental health and experiences during lockdown.

Teachers from the 85 schools taking part in the study were also surveyed on the words they use most often when talking to children about their physical and mental health.

More than one in five (21 per cent) students said 'anxiety' was the word they identified with most during the past year, closely followed by 'challenging' (19 per cent) and 'isolate' (14 per cent).

Experts said the findings highlight the impact that lockdown and school closures had on children, and the 'vital role language plays for children when it comes to self-expression, learning and wellbeing'.

'It's important now, more than ever, that we invest in supporting children's language development at home and in school,' Helen Freeman, director of early childhood and home education at OUP, said.

'The findings demonstrate the role we all play in making sure children have the words they need to be able to express themselves and that, as adults, we are aware the language we use around children can significantly influence their learning and wellbeing.'

The news comes as OUP prepares to update its dictionaries and resources for schools with new phrases and definitions for popular words during the pandemic, such as 'bubble', 'lockdown' and 'self-isolation'.

Of the teachers who took part in the survey, 31 per cent said 'resilience' was the word they used most when talking to their pupils about the pandemic, a finding which lexicographers said reflects the importance of providing children with positive direction.

The second most used word was 'challenging', followed by 'wellbeing'.

Joe Jenkins, the executive director of social impact at The Children's Society, commented: 'It's concerning that "anxiety" is the number one word but it isn't surprising when you consider all the restrictions and changes children had to endure.

'Having conversations and using the right language is incredibly important when supporting children if they are feeling anxious, isolated or going through tough challenges, and it's also crucial children are able to express how they are feeling.'

The charity's *Good Childhood Report*, published in August 2021, estimated that more than 300,000 children in the UK felt unhappy with their lives in 2018-2019.

While most children surveyed said they had adjusted well to changes to daily life under lockdown and social restrictions, they coped less well with not being able to take part in hobbies and see friends and family.

Last year's Children's Word of the Year was coronavirus, and in 2019 it was Brexit.

*18 January 2022*

Additional reporting by PA

The above information is reprinted with kind permission from *The Independent*.
© independent.co.uk 2023

www.independent.co.uk

# Anxiety and panic attacks

## What causes anxiety?

Everyone's experience of anxiety is different, so it's hard to know exactly what causes anxiety problems. There are probably lots of factors involved.

This page covers some things which make anxiety problems more likely to happen:

- past or childhood experiences
- your current life situation
- physical and mental health problems
- drugs and medication

## Can anxiety problems be inherited genetically?

Research shows that having a close relative with anxiety problems might increase your chances of experiencing anxiety problems yourself. This is sometimes called 'anxiety sensitivity'.

At the moment there is not enough evidence to show whether this is because we share some genes that make us more vulnerable to developing anxiety, or because we learn particular ways of thinking and behaving from our parents and other family members as we grow up.

## Past or childhood experiences

Difficult experiences in childhood, adolescence or adulthood are a common trigger for anxiety problems. Going through stress and trauma when you're very young is likely to have a particularly big impact. Experiences which can trigger anxiety problems include things like:

- physical or emotional abuse
- neglect
- losing a parent
- being bullied or being socially excluded
- experiencing racism.

Having parents who don't treat you warmly or are overprotective can also be a factor.

> 'I was sent to boarding school and suffered acute separation anxiety, being away from home, and my brother nearly died when I was 12. My mum had an acute breakdown for a period of about a year and had to be home-nursed.'

## Your current life situation

Current problems in your life can also trigger anxiety. For example:

- exhaustion or a build-up of stress
- lots of change or uncertainty
- feeling under pressure while studying or in work
- long working hours
- being out of work
- money problems
- housing problems and homelessness
- worrying about the environment or natural disasters (sometimes called climate anxiety or eco-anxiety)
- losing someone close to you (sometimes called bereavement)
- feeling lonely or isolated
- being abused, bullied or harassed, including experiencing racism.

Big changes to your day-to-day life can be a particular trigger for anxiety, so you may find that you've experienced anxiety problems during the coronavirus pandemic.

> 'I have recently realised that I spend money when anxious, which in turn makes me feel anxious about how much I'm spending.'

## Physical or mental health problems

Other health problems can sometimes cause anxiety, or might make it worse. For example:

- **Physical health problems** – living with a serious, ongoing or life-threatening physical health condition can sometimes trigger anxiety.
- **Other mental health problems** – it's also common to develop anxiety while living with other mental health problems, such as depression.

## Drugs and medication

Anxiety can sometimes be a side effect of taking:

- some psychiatric medications
- some medications for physical health problems
- recreational drugs and alcohol.

## Could diet be a factor?

Some types of food or drink can trigger symptoms of anxiety or panic, or make them worse. These include sugar and caffeine. See our pages on food and mood for more information about the relationship between what you eat and how you feel.

> 'I had cut out alcohol. Many think drinking alcohol helps with anxiety, but it actually makes it worse in the long run.'

*February 2021*

The above information is reprinted with kind permission from Mind.
This information is published in full at mind.org.uk
© 2023 Mind

www.mind.org.uk

# Anxiety, fear and panic

Most people feel anxious or scared sometimes, but if it's affecting your life there are things you can try that may help.

Support is also available if you're finding it hard to cope with anxiety, fear or panic.

## Symptoms of anxiety

Anxiety can cause many different symptoms. It might affect how you feel physically, mentally and how you behave.

It's not always easy to recognise when anxiety is the reason you're feeling or acting differently.

**Physical symptoms**

- faster, irregular or more noticeable heartbeat
- feeling lightheaded and dizzy
- headaches
- chest pains
- loss of appetite
- sweating
- breathlessness
- feeling hot
- shaking

**Mental symptoms**

- feeling tense or nervous
- being unable to relax
- worrying about the past or future
- feeling tearful
- not being able to sleep
- difficulty concentrating
- fear of the worst happening
- intrusive traumatic memories
- obsessive thoughts

**Changes in behaviour**

- not being able to enjoy your leisure time
- difficulty looking after yourself
- struggling to form or maintain relationships
- worried about trying new things
- avoiding places and situations that create anxiety
- compulsive behaviour, such as constantly checking things

## Symptoms of a panic attack

If you experience sudden, intense anxiety and fear, it might be the symptoms of a panic attack. Other symptoms may include:

- a racing heartbeat
- feeling faint, dizzy or lightheaded
- feeling that you're losing control
- sweating, trembling or shaking
- shortness of breath or breathing very quickly
- a tingling in your fingers or lips
- feeling sick (nausea)

A panic attack usually lasts 5 to 30 minutes. They can be frightening, but they're not dangerous and should not harm you.

Things you can try to help with anxiety, fear and panic

**Do**

- try talking about your feelings to a friend, family member, health professional or counsellor. You could also contact Samaritans, call: 116 123 or email: jo@samaritans.org if you need someone to talk to
- use calming breathing exercises
- exercise – activities such as running, walking, swimming and yoga can help you relax
- find out how to get to sleep if you're struggling to sleep
- eat a healthy diet with regular meals to keep your energy levels stable
- consider peer support, where people use their experiences to help each other. Find out more about peer support on the Mind website
- listen to free mental wellbeing audio guides

**Don't**

- do not try to do everything at once – set small targets that you can easily achieve
- do not focus on the things you cannot change – focus your time and energy into helping yourself feel better
- do not avoid situations that make you anxious – try slowly building up time spent in worrying situations to gradually reduce anxiety
- try not to tell yourself that you're alone; most people experience anxiety or fear at some point in their life
- try not to use alcohol, cigarettes, gambling or drugs to relieve anxiety as these can all contribute to poor mental health

## Causes of anxiety, fear and panic

There are many different causes of anxiety, fear or panic and it's different for everyone.

When you're feeling anxious or scared, your body releases stress hormones, such as adrenaline and cortisol.

This can be helpful in some situations, but it might also cause physical symptoms such as an increased heart rate and increased sweating. In some people, it might cause a panic attack.

Regular anxiety, fear or panic can also be the main symptom of several health conditions. Do not self-diagnose – speak to a GP if you're worried about how you're feeling.

## Identifying the cause

If you know what's causing anxiety, fear or panic, it might be easier to find ways to manage it.

Some examples of possible causes include:

- work – feeling pressure at work, unemployment or retirement
- family – relationship difficulties, divorce or caring for someone
- financial problems – unexpected bills or borrowing money
- health – illness, injury or losing someone (bereavement)
- difficult past experiences – bullying, abuse or neglect

Even significant life events such as buying a house, having a baby or planning a wedding could lead to feelings of stress and anxiety.

You might find it hard to explain to people why you feel this way, but talking to someone could help you find a solution.

*17 January 2023*

The above information is reprinted with kind permission from the NHS.
© Crown Copyright 2023
This information is licensed under the Open Government Licence v3.0
To view this licence, visit http://www.nationalarchives.gov.uk/doc/open-government-licence/

www.nhs.uk

# From jubbity to mubble fubbles, anxiety is well catered for in the historical dictionary

The story of the word anxiety itself gives us a sense of the chokehold that worry can bring.

By Susie Dent

Confused tremor and fremescence; waxing into thunderpeals, of Fury stirred on by Fear.' In his history of the French Revolution, Thomas Carlyle charted the build-up of frustration and anxiety that was to eventually erupt inexorably. He was the first to give us the term 'fremescence', a description of 'an incipient roaring'. In other words, this was a growing sense of dissatisfaction that could only go one way. Some of us may be aware of a similarly low roar now, as we approach the autumn with dread over rising prices, continuing war on our doorsteps, and the unknown quantity of a new Prime Minister to navigate us (or not) through it all. If ever we needed to borrow from the lexicon of unease, it's probably now.

Anxiety is well catered for in the historical dictionary. The story of that word itself, from the Latin *angere*, to 'strangle', gives us a sense of the chokehold that worry can bring. Before 'unease' we had 'disease', originally an absence of comfort (a 'dis-ease') before settling on the causes of such disturbances. Those causes were often viewed as outside human control. The stars in particular were believed to exert enormous influence over human affairs and our feelings. The word 'disaster', close to a lot of our lips at the moment, revolves around the Latin *aster*, 'star', for a truly calamitous event was thought to come from an unlucky alignment of the constellations. Similarly, 'influenza', from the Italian for 'influence', was viewed as the direct result of astral influence.

No one needs to look to the stars to find the causes of collective unease right now. The catalysts for societal jitters have of course varied widely over the centuries. In the sixteenth and seventeenth centuries, the authorities were particularly eager to identify those prone to anxiety, such as witches, or women with a 'wandering' uterus thought susceptible to bouts of hysteria (from the Greek *hystera*, 'womb'). In the nineteenth century, among the biggest catalysts of widespread anxiety was the fear of being buried alive, thanks to shaky diagnostics and in-fighting between medics and undertakers as to who had the authority to certify death. Various cures for such predicaments were experimented with, from supplying coffins with bells, to coaxing the recalcitrant uterus back into normal position by wafting unpleasant smells near the vagina. You'd think that financial support from a whiffling government might seem a little less onerous.

There is of course a cuddlier side to anxiety, linguistically at least, as anyone who has the screaming abdabs or heebie-jeebies will agree. A 'jubbity', in Yorkshire dialect, is a misfortune or vexatious experience, as in 'she's had some jubbities in her life'. To have a jittery kind of melancholy, meanwhile, or a sense of impending doom – as of a Sunday evening or the day your energy bill is due – was disarmingly known in the 17th century as the 'mubble fubbles'. 'Having the morbs', Victorian style, was to sit under a cloud of despondency – an expression that sits nicely alongside another, shoulder-shrugging offering of the time, 'Damfino', short for 'damned if I know'.

For acuter anxiety however, because damned if any of us know how to slam the brakes on the train hurtling towards us at the moment, there are familiar words such as 'funked' and 'perturbed', and those less travelled, like 'bumbazed', 'bogfoundered', and 'forstraught'. For an expression of utter befuddlement and shock, there is the 19th- century dialect term 'blutterbunged'.

In Old English, the act of lying awake and contemplating the enormity of life and its worries was known as 'uhtcearu', the 'sorrow before dawn'. A now-lost Irish equivalent is 'iarmhaireacht', exquisitely described by the writer Manchán Magan as 'the loneliness you feel at cockcrow, when you are the only person awake and experience that existential pang of disconnection, of not belonging'. Such feeling is often followed up by 'matutolypea', a morning irritability when we can just about manage to trampoose to the kettle but woe betide anyone who dares speak to us.

The fact that our language can provide us with a long trail of words with which to express our unease may offer some consolation, if little remedy. If you were to ask the Romans, one strategy for a dissatisfied audience was 'exsibilation', the act of hissing a poor performer off the stage. But while poor performers abound, we'd need a lot of hissing to get anywhere. And all the while that slow-building roar is getting a little louder. Listen out for 'brontide', the low, muffled sound of distant thunder. How long before Fury stirred on by Fear takes over once again?

*1 September 2022*

Susie Dent is a lexicographer and etymologist. She has appeared in 'Dictionary Corner' on Countdown since 1992, and co-hosts with Gyles Brandreth the podcast Something Rhymes with Purple.

---

### Write

Write a short definition of each of the following:

- General anxiety disorder (GAD)
- Social anxiety
- Panic disorder
- Clinical depression

The above information is reprinted with kind permission from i News.
© 2023 Associated Newspapers Limited

www.inews.co.uk

# Anxiety in autistic children – why rates are so high

An article from The Conversation.

Keren MacLennan, Doctoral Researcher, Autism, University of Reading

Many aspects of the world can be overwhelming for autistic children, so it is unsurprising that dealing with the challenging impact of anxiety has become a daily struggle for many autistic children and their families. In fact, autistic children are twice as likely to develop anxiety than non-autistic children. Not only this, but around 40% are diagnosed with at least one anxiety disorder, with the most common being specific phobia, which is an extreme fear of a particular place, object, animal, person or situation.

Many autistic people carry this disabling anxiety into adulthood, which can negatively affect their future prospects and quality of life. Because of this, autism researchers have made it a priority to understand why autistic children are much more at risk of developing anxiety and what can be done to prevent it.

Sensory hyper-reactivity, such as being over-responsive to loud noises, bright lights and clothing fabrics, has been suggested as a reason autistic children develop anxiety. It is commonly experienced by autistic children and has recently become one of the criteria for an autism diagnosis.

Autistic children can struggle to filter out and ignore things they hear, see, touch, smell and taste. This can lead to them feeling exhausted, stressed and overwhelmed, which in turn, can increase sensory hyper-reactivity, creating a vicious cycle of anxiety due to sensory difficulties and sensory difficulties due to anxiety.

Existing research indicates that sensory difficulties are one of the reasons autistic children are more anxious in a general sense. But when considering targeted therapies, we really need to know if sensory hyper-reactivity is more strongly linked to particular anxiety disorders, such as generalised anxiety disorder (feeling anxious about a wide range of situations) or social anxiety disorder (overwhelming fear of social situations).

This is important for understanding how to create strategies that prevent different anxiety disorders. That is why our recent study investigated the relationship between sensory hyper-reactivity and anxiety in more detail.

## Finding the link

At the University of Reading's Centre for Autism, we assessed sensory hyper-reactivity and anxiety in 41 autistic children, aged three to 14 years. All of the children had a formal diagnosis of autism and had average to above-average IQs. Parents completed questionnaires that told us the extent of their children's sensory hyper-reactivity and anxiety. We also gave a questionnaire to children aged six years and over so they could rate their anxiety.

We found that autistic children who were more sensory hyper-reactive also had greater overall anxiety, as well as more symptoms relating to phobia and separation anxiety disorder. This tells us that sensory hyper-reactivity is related to anxiety in a general sense, but it may be more strongly linked to some anxiety disorders, and less so to others.

Yet we know that other autism traits, such as repetitive behaviours, have also been linked to anxiety, so we repeated the analysis controlling for broader autism traits. We could then see if our results changed when taking these into account.

We found that autistic children who were more sensory hyper-reactive also had more symptoms associated with phobia. But we no longer found sensory hyper-reactivity to be related to overall anxiety or separation anxiety. This tells us that other autism traits, together with sensory hyper-reactivity, may be why autistic children are more likely to be anxious. But sensory hyper-reactivity could be more specifically linked to symptoms of phobia.

## Early intervention

There are existing therapies to help autistic children deal with their anxiety. But it would be better to combat any risk factors before these anxiety disorders have a chance to develop. For example, if an autistic child struggles with sudden loud noises at an early age, this may evolve into them developing a fear of things that produce these sounds, such as dogs because of their barking, or balloons, due to them popping.

If we can address sensory hyper-reactivity early on in autistic children, this might prevent them from developing phobias later in life. But how do we do this?

Sensory difficulties are often addressed using a range of approaches through occupational therapy. But it is not clear how effective these approaches are in tackling anxiety.

As there is much individual difference in autism, with a range of strengths and difficulties, taking a personalised approach to helping autistic children may be the most effective method to prevent anxiety. So this may be key to developing effective, evidence-based therapies to improve the lives and future prospects of these autistic children.

*14 February 2020*

**THE CONVERSATION**

The above information is reprinted with kind permission from The Conversation.
© 2010-2023, The Conversation Trust (UK) Limited

www.theconversation.com

# Anxiety statistics 2023

Data collected from The Workplace Health Report 2023.

By Joe Pindar

There has been an 'explosion' in anxiety across Britain over the last decade, according to research, but just how prevalent is it really? To learn more, we're going to dive into the data and explore anxiety statistics in the UK.

Anxiety is a future-oriented state of mind, characterised by feelings of fear, worry or general unease. Everyone feels anxious from time to time, but for some, their anxiety is constant and affects their daily lives.

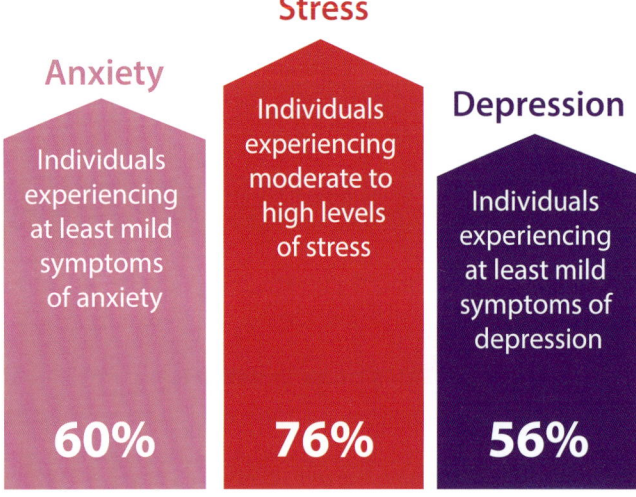

### Mental health & wellbeing in 2023

- **Anxiety**: Individuals experiencing at least mild symptoms of anxiety — **60%**
- **Stress**: Individuals experiencing moderate to high levels of stress — **76%**
- **Depression**: Individuals experiencing at least mild symptoms of depression — **56%**

*Data from Champion Health. Sample size: 4170 individuals.*

As we continue to navigate an uncertain world, our mental wellbeing is constantly being tested, which has led to levels of anxiety increasing around the world. In the UK, anxiety is among the most common mental health disorders.

Research also shows that employee anxiety is a challenge facing organisations, with anxiety accounting for a significant percentage of all work-related ill health cases.

Part of understanding anxiety is educating ourselves on current data and research around the topic. Read on to discover anxiety statistics, in the workplace and beyond, from leading organisations in mental health, academia and public health.

## Anxiety Statistics UK

Exploring UK anxiety statistics reveals how many people need support, and the extent to which different demographics are affected by anxiety.

The research shows that:

- In any given week in England, 6 in 100 people will be diagnosed with generalised anxiety disorder (Mind)
- In the UK, over 8 million people are experiencing an anxiety disorder at any one time (Mental Health UK)
- Less than 50% of people with generalised anxiety disorder access treatment (Mental Health Foundation)
- An estimated 822,000 workers are affected by work-related stress, depression or anxiety every year (Health and Safety Executive)

With so many employees experiencing anxiety, organisations must also be aware of how anxiety will impact their people's wellbeing. With that in mind, read on to explore employee anxiety statistics.

## Employee anxiety statistics

This year, the experts at Champion Health revealed the impact of anxiety on UK employees in The Workplace Health Report.

The Champion team set out to discover the health challenges faced by the UK's workforce, from mental health, to sleep quality, productivity, musculoskeletal health and beyond.

The result was a range of employee anxiety statistics which highlighted, among other things, these four key findings:

1. 60% of employees are experiencing anxiety
2. 67% of employees aged 16-24 are experiencing anxiety
3. 65% of females are experiencing anxiety
4. Only 10% of employees are seeking mental health support

### 1. Symptoms of anxiety are prevalent among UK employees

Champion's data found that, across the board, the number of employees experiencing symptoms of anxiety remains high; 58% of employees are experiencing at least mild symptoms of anxiety.

Almost a quarter of employees are also experiencing 'clinically relevant symptoms', suggesting that they would benefit from a qualified medical health professional.

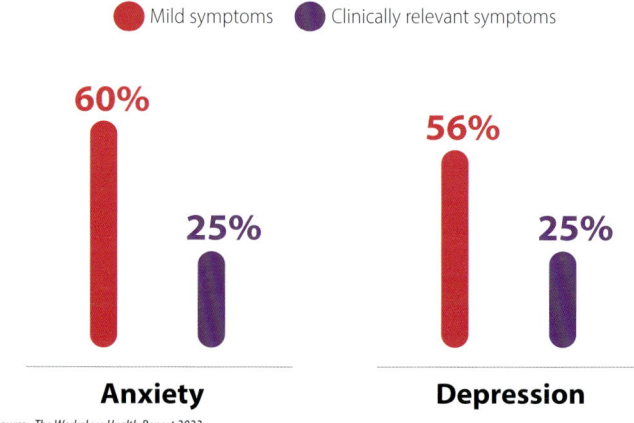

### Employees experiencing symptoms of anxiety and depression

Symptoms of anxiety and depression as measured by the GAD-7 and PHQ-9. Mild symptoms defined as scoring ≥5. Clinically relevant symptoms defined as scoring ≥10.

- Mild symptoms / Clinically relevant symptoms
- Anxiety: 60% / 25%
- Depression: 56% / 25%

*Source: The Workplace Health Report 2023*

## 2. Younger employees are being affected more by anxiety

Champion's research also revealed that younger employees are more likely to experience anxiety compared to their older colleagues.

For employees aged between 16-24, 67% reported experiencing symptoms of anxiety. We found a similar link between age of employee and depression, which you can read more about in this article on depression statistics.

Employees aged between 25 and 34 were the next most affected group, with 66% of the age range reporting symptoms of mild-to-severe anxiety.

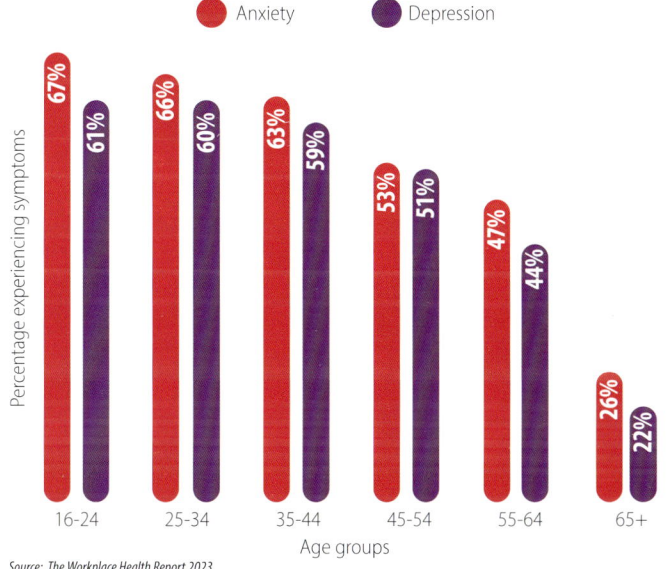

Source: The Workplace Health Report 2023

These findings take on greater significance when considered alongside research by Deloitte, which suggested that pandemic-related worries, such as job security and the resulting financial pressure, are more likely to impact younger employees.

## 3. Levels of anxiety are higher among female employees

Champion's research also revealed that female employees are more likely to experience symptoms of anxiety than male employees. Almost two-thirds of women are experiencing anxiety.

More research by Deloitte may point to the reasons for this pattern. Their findings indicate that female professionals have fared poorer throughout the pandemic, due to factors such as increased workloads and household responsibilities.

The discrepancies between different employee demographics highlights the need for leaders to recognise the different pressures faced by different employees and commit to addressing them.

## 4. Employees aren't seeking mental health support

Despite the prevalence of anxiety and depression among UK professionals, Champion's data also revealed a reluctance around employees to engage with mental health support.

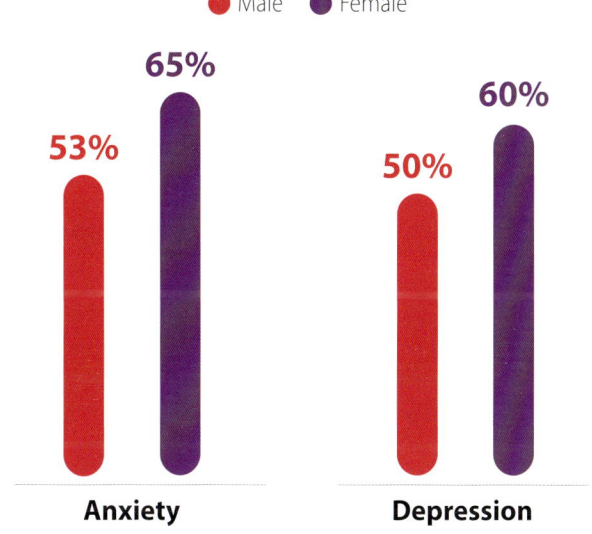

Source: The Workplace Health Report 2023

Just 1 in 10 employees are currently seeking support for their mental health, including counselling, talking therapies and medication. This is despite 19% reporting a current mental health diagnosis.

These statistics highlight the importance of employers being proactive about employee mental health, to get their people the right help at the right time.

It's essential that people managers can spot the signs of struggling employees, and provide them with the appropriate reasonable adjustments.

### Anxiety statistics: painting a concerning picture

The statistics outlined in this article highlight the scale of the public health challenge posed by anxiety, and the key role employers must play in meeting that challenge.

With nearly 60% of employees experiencing symptoms of anxiety, proactively managing employee mental health must be at the forefront of any successful workplace health strategy.

There are many ways that leaders can support employees with anxiety, including:

- Bringing up mental health in 1:1s and staff appraisals
- Taking steps to reduce workplace stress
- Signposting towards internal wellbeing offerings (such as EAPs) and external support services

Uncertainty may be a normal part of life, but with rates of anxiety increasing across the UK, we must all do more to support our colleagues, friends and family.

*15 February 2023*

The above information is reprinted with kind permission from Champion Health.
© 2023 Champion Health

www.championhealth.co.uk

# Young lives under pressure as global crises hits mental health and well-being – report

The well-being and mental health of young people in low- and middle-income countries have been dramatically affected by the series of crises hitting the world.

As the international community continues to struggle with the impact of COVID-19, conflict and climate change, the latest report from the Young Lives project shows a long- running upward trend in young people's well-being has been sharply reversed alongside widespread anxiety and depression. Young people are less confident about their futures for the first time in the 20-year study.

Before the pandemic, there had been a steady but notable upward trend in young people's sense of well-being across all four countries in the Young Lives study – Peru, Vietnam, India and Ethiopia. But new data from the most recent survey, collected during the pandemic, shows young people reported a significant decline in well-being – and high levels of anxiety and depression.

The latest report shows global crises are triggering mental health issues among disadvantaged youth at a critical period in their lives – because long-term mental health issues often begin in adolescence and early adulthood. Many countries are ill-equipped to manage this wave of anxiety and depression, as mental health support services for young people are hugely underfunded around the world – especially in poorer countries, where there is often an acute shortage of mental health specialists.

*'New data shows young people reported a significant decline in well-being - and high levels of anxiety and depression…at a critical period in [young] lives - because long-term mental health issues often begin in adolescence and early adulthood'*

'We are very concerned about the long-term impact of declining well-being and widespread anxiety and depression across our study countries. Urgent action is needed to protect, promote and care for young people's mental health, particularly those from disadvantaged backgrounds,' says Kath Ford, Senior Policy Officer, Young Lives and lead author of the new report.

One factor, which seems to have protected some young people from mental health issues over the last two years, has been close family relationships and friendships. In Peru, young people, who did not have a strong relationship with their parents before the pandemic, experienced significantly higher symptoms of depression (36%) than those who had a strong parental relationship (28%).

*Young Lives* has followed 12,000 young people across two age cohorts over 20 years. During the pandemic, researchers interviewed them five times by phone and found:

Young people's mental health worsened as the pandemic became more severe. In 2020, Peru had one of the highest death rates from COVID-19 in the world. After the first months of the pandemic, 40% of young people reported symptoms of anxiety and 30% reported symptoms of depression (compared to 18% experiencing depression in 2019).

Vietnam was very successful in limiting infections throughout 2020 – and in that year just 5% of young people reported symptoms of anxiety and 6% reported symptoms of depression.

The stress and loneliness of prolonged school and university closures, and uncertainty surrounding the virus, affected young people's well-being and mental health. Young women's mental health was disproportionately affected by interrupted education and also by increased domestic work associated with the pandemic.

> *'I feel very stressed when I am at home... I mean for virtual classes and all that. I have anxiety when I am at home.'*
>
> (Daniela, female university student from rural Peru, 2021)

Job losses also caused widespread anxiety for young people with those who lost their jobs most likely to experience symptoms of anxiety in all four study countries. In India, those who lost their jobs were twice as likely to report anxiety.

Young people are often coping with multiple, intersecting crises. In all countries, persistent food insecurity was found to be taking a toll on young people's mental health, exacerbated by the pandemic but also by conflict and climate-related shocks such as severe drought in Ethiopia.

### Key Facts

- In 2020, Peru had one of the highest death rates from COVID-19 in the world. After the first few months of the pandemic 40% of young people reported symptoms of anxiety and 30% reported symptoms of depression (compared to 18% experiencing depression in 2019).
- Vietnam was successful in limiting COVID-19 infections throughout 2020 – in that year just 5% of young people reported symptoms of anxiety and 6% reported symptoms of depression.

The evidence shows young people were increasingly worried about running out of food during 2021, with those from poorer and marginalised groups most affected. In Ethiopia, the on-going conflict in Tigray was an additional threat to young people's mental health.

Two out of five young people in Tigray experienced mental health issues in the initial months after the start of the conflict with rates of depression increasing from 16 to 25%.

Young men experienced greater anxiety, whilst young women were more at risk of increased depression.

'A significant increase in global investment in young people's mental health is critical to support developing countries in meeting the Sustainable Development Goal target on promoting mental health and well-being for all ages. Priority should be given to measures which mainstream and integrate mental health care into existing services at the community level, as well as to break the silence around mental health issues,' says Kath Ford.

Young Lives will return to the field in 2023 to gather new data and insights on the medium-term impact of the pandemic on young people's mental health and well-being, alongside the compounding effects of increasing food insecurity and the ongoing conflict in Ethiopia.

*23 November 2022*

Full report available here: Ford, K., and R. Freund (2022) *Young Lives Under Pressure: Protecting and Promoting Young People's Mental Health at a Time of Global Crises*, Young Lives Policy Brief 55, Oxford: Young Lives.

### Activity

As a class, make a list of the biggest global events currently in the news. Discuss which events you consider the cause for most concern, and why.

*The Young Lives study is based at the Department of International Development, University of Oxford*
*The above information is reprinted with kind permission from Young Lives, University of Oxford*
*© Young Lives 2023*

**www.ox.ac.uk**

# Why anxiety can be good for you – even if it feels terrible

Rather than avoiding it at all costs, we should harness the emotion in a positive way, says a new book.

By Marianne Power

I once read that people who get depressed tend to live in the past, while people who suffer from anxiety spend their days imagining the future. That made sense to me.

As a depressive sort, I can spend many an hour reliving everything I've ever done wrong, ever. As hobbies go, I wouldn't recommend it. But in lockdown I picked up an exciting new one: sitting bolt upright in bed at 3am, heart pounding, with a sense that something terrible was about to happen. What, I didn't know.

The pounding heart came back when I'd write an article. What if there were a mistake in it? What if I were sued? If friends didn't text back immediately, I panicked that I'd done something wrong. Contrarily, I would also panic if I got a message asking if I was around to chat. What had I done?

Having spent years not really understanding anxiety, I've now had a taste of it and I'm not a fan. But a new book says I should be.

*Future Tense: Why Anxiety Is Good for You (Even Though it Feels Bad)*, by psychologist Tracy Dennis-Tiwary, argues that far from being a 'bad' feeling that we need to suppress, anxiety is our friend, alerting us to things that need addressing and giving us the energy to do just that. Anxiety might not feel good, but, she argues, it's actually trying to help us.

'We mental-health professionals have promulgated this idea that any experience of anxiety is dangerous and potentially a disease, so we have to eradicate it and avoid it and suppress it and soothe it. But that's the opposite of what you should do,' says Dr. Dennis-Tiwary.

She explains that emotions are there for a reason. If we are angry, it's because somebody or something is getting in our way, and we need to defend ourselves. If we are anxious, it's because there is something we need to do to prepare for the future.

We are living in an age of anxiety. Even before the pandemic, one of the biggest pieces of research done into anxiety in this country showed that the UK had experienced an 'explosion' of anxiety since 2008.

The financial crash, austerity, Brexit, climate change and social media were blamed for the rise. The figures ended just before the pandemic began, when, unsurprisingly, anxiety rose even further. In the UK, prescriptions for anti-anxiety medications have almost doubled over the past 15 years, with a sharp rise amongst under-25s.

But could it be that we need to rethink anxiety? Is it really possible to see it as a friend rather than a foe?

First of all, we need to differentiate anxiety from fear.

'Fear is about present threats – for example, if a snake is about to bite you. You are certain that there is a present danger and your body responds with fight or flight, so that you can protect yourself. Anxiety has nothing to do with the present moment – it is all about the future. It's using one of our greatest human attributes, which is to think about the future and imagine all the possibilities – both good and bad,' explains Dr. Dennis-Tiwary. Anxiety is an emotion distinct from anxiety disorders, she says.

'We might have intense anxiety, but that's not the same as an anxiety disorder, which is when our ways of coping with anxiety are disrupting our ability to live life.'

So, if we're socially anxious and our way of coping with that is by no longer going out, that's a disorder. Being nervous about going out is not a disorder.

Anxiety is on a spectrum, says Dr. Dennis-Tiwary. Everyday anxiety is there to help us and we should be listening to it, not running away from it.

'Say you're up at 5am, with free-floating anxiety. If you have the view that anxiety is a problem, you'll ignore it. You'll get

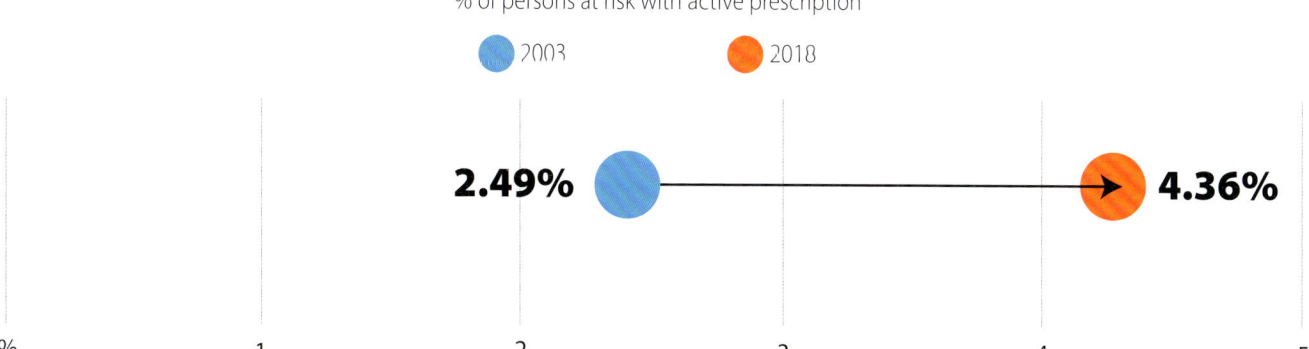

up and try to do something else. Or you take medication – which can be helpful sometimes – but you won't hear what it has to say. But what if you sat there and asked anxiety what it has for you. 'Could it be about the argument I had with my husband last night? No, we resolved that… Could it be the deadline looming? No, that's in hand…' And then you're like, 'Oh, wait a second, I've been trying not to accept that I've been waking up with stomach pains every morning. I need to investigate this.' '

So, anxiety's job is to alert us to a problem and then give us the chemical drive to do something.

'There is excellent evidence that shows that it makes us more productive, more creative, more innovative. There's a study where people were asked to write about something anxiety-provoking in their own life, while some wrote about things that made them happy and angry. Then they were asked to do a problem-solving task. They found that the people who felt more anxious were actually more persistent in problem-solving. And they were actually more creative – they came up with more ideas of a higher quality.'

The pounding heart of anxiety is pumping oxygen to the brain, so that we can think more clearly. Anxiety also boosts the social-bonding hormone oxytocin, which makes us seek connection.

Dr. Dennis-Tiwary adds: 'Anxiety also boosts dopamine, which is the feel-good hormone. One of its most important functions is to help us pursue goals, so if there is something important we want to achieve, dopamine starts to activate. It is not just about averting disasters, it's about pursuing positive possibilities. The biology of anxiety prepares us for that.'

The story we tell ourselves about our anxiety is important, as demonstrated by a trial where socially anxious people were asked to give an impromptu talk to a panel of judges who had been told to look uninterested. The people were split into two groups. The first was just sent straight in. The second group was given a pep talk first, where it was explained to them that their anxiety was actually helping them to perform better.

After the test, the people who had had the pep talk had lower blood pressure, their heart rate was slower and calmer, and they had performed better.

But what if you are anxious for no reason? Nobody is sick, there's enough to pay the bills – and still your heart is pounding and your thoughts are racing?

'Sometimes, we are just on high alert and we don't find a specific reason for it,' says Dr. Dennis-Tiwary. 'Sometimes, being on high alert can become a habit, we get stuck in a worry loop.'

If that is the case, there are a few things we can do. First, we should cut back on caffeine and alcohol, and increase our exercise. Next, if your mind is constantly going into the future, find ways to be here, in this moment. Mindfulness meditation helps, as does any kind of exercise, being in nature, gardening or listening to music. Writing a to-do list can help us to feel some sense of control.

Cognitive behavioural therapy is considered the gold standard for anxiety. This kind of therapy helps you to understand your behaviour and gives you the tools to do things differently. Medication can also help, alongside therapy.

But the worst thing we can do with anxiety is to try to suppress it.

She worries about the lengths we are going to to avoid anxiety in society: with trigger warnings, safe spaces and the rise of 'snowplough' parenting, when parents try to remove all obstacles from their children's lives.

This avoidance builds a sense that we are weak and unable to cope with difficult things – which is not true.

'Our emotional systems are like our immune system,' she explains. 'If our immune system isn't exposed to germs, it remains weak. If our muscles aren't used, they atrophy. It's only by feeling our anxiety – listening and acting on it – that we can cope better next time.'

If anxiety is a beeping smoke alarm, my approach has been to rip it down, wrap it in a duvet and hide it. It's time to face up to what the beeping is about.

I have some ideas about what's going on: financial worries, strained friendships, an uncertain future in a world that seems to be imploding. It can feel like so much is out of our control, but there are small things that we can do – whether it's calling a friend, writing a to-do list or cutting down on coffee. I'm lucky, my anxiety is very mild compared to what many live with, but I don't want to ignore it any more.

Perhaps anxiety can be a call to action. Yes, there may be difficult times ahead, but if I take my head out of the sand and do what needs to be done, there might be some good times, too.

## Other bad feelings that may be good too

### Regret

In *The Power of Regret*, author Daniel Pink writes that Edith Piaf had it wrong. Regrets are helpful if we learn from them. In two large surveys he found that people's regrets fall into four categories.

First, people regret failure to act boldly – to not get on that plane, or take that job. Then came moral regrets about the times people were unkind, lied and bullied. People also regretted letting contact with loved ones fall away. And had foundational regrets about their failure to be responsible or prudent.

Ignoring regrets means we don't learn – but wallowing in them paralyses us. The answer is in the middle, having the courage to face our mistakes and make amends, where possible, by apologising or rectifying the behaviour. You could try writing a 'failure CV', which is where you list your mistakes in one column and in the next column list what you've learnt from them.

### Anger

Research suggests that feeling angry increases optimism, creativity, effective performance – and expressing anger can lead to more successful negotiations, at home or at work. Like all emotions, it serves a purpose: it gives you the energy to face an adversary or a challenge. In fact, repressing anger can actually hurt you.

### Sadness

*Bittersweet* by Susan Cain explains that melancholy feelings such as sadness, longing and grief are vital parts of being human, leading to great creativity and connection. When we see someone is sad, our first instinct is to help them, so it's a helpful way for us to come together. What's more, sadness is often the source of inspiration for great art and music. Apparently, people listen to happy songs on their playlists about 175 times, but sad ones 800 times. They say happy songs make them happy, but sad ones make them feel connected, full.

*29 May 2022*

### Key Facts

- Even before the pandemic, one of the biggest pieces of research done into anxiety in this country showed that the UK had experienced an 'explosion' of anxiety since 2008.
- In the UK, prescriptions for anti-anxiety medications have almost doubled over the past 15 years, with a sharp rise amongst under-25s.

### Create

Create either an illustration or infograph highlighting the key points raised in this article.

The above information is reprinted with kind permission from *The Telegraph*.
© Telegraph Media Group Limited 2022

www.telegraph.co.uk

# Depression, anxiety and heart disease risk all linked to single brain region

An article from The Conversation.

By Laith Alexander, Academic Foundation Doctor, University of Cambridge; Angela Charlotte Roberts, Professor of Behavioural Neuroscience, University of Cambridge & Christian Wood, Postdoctoral Research Associate, Physiology and Pharmacology, University of Cambridge

Although depression and anxiety affect millions of people worldwide, there's still much we don't know about them. In fact, we still don't fully understand which brain regions are involved in depression and anxiety, and how they differ between people with varying symptoms. Understanding how or why these differences occur is fundamental to developing better treatments.

So far, we know that part of the brain's frontal lobe, the prefrontal cortex, often shows activity changes in people with depression and anxiety. Parts involved in cognition and regulating emotions are underactive, whereas other parts involved in emotion generation and internal bodily functions are over-active.

One key region shown to be over-active in people with depression and anxiety is the subgenual anterior cingulate cortex (sgACC), thought to be involved in emotional responses. However, neuroimaging studies only show correlation and don't tell us that the over-activity causes any of the symptoms. But our new research has found over-activating the sgACC induces symptoms of depression and anxiety, highlighting causality.

For our study, we used marmosets (a type of primate) because their brain closely resembles a human's brain. We found over-activity in this region causes several key features of mood and anxiety disorders, particularly how reactive they are to threat. Their reaction to threat is important, as patients with depression and anxiety tend to perceive and react to situations more negatively.

To over-activate sgACC, we implanted tiny hollow tubes – called cannulae – into the marmosets' brains. We then infused small amounts of a drug into sgACC to increase excitability without damaging or disrupting function in other brain regions. We also implanted a small wireless device into an artery to measure blood pressure and heart rate.

But before over-activating sgACC, we trained the marmosets to associate a specific tone with the presence of a rubber snake, which marmosets find threatening. After learning this association, the marmosets exhibited fear and had higher blood pressure when hearing the tone. We then presented the tone without the snake to break this association. This allowed us to measure how quickly the marmosets could

> **Key Facts**
> - The brain's frontal lobe, the prefrontal cortex, often shows activity changes in people with depression and anxiety. Parts involved in cognition and regulating emotions are underactive, whereas other parts involved in emotion generation and internal bodily functions are over-active.
> - One key region shown to be over-active in people with depression and anxiety is the subgenual anterior cingulate cortex (sgACC), thought to be involved in emotional responses.
> - People with depression also have increased risk of heart disease.
> - The most common type of antidepressants are selective serotonin re-uptake inhibitors (SSRIs).

dampen their fear response with and without sgACC over-activation.

Without over-activation, marmosets gradually regulated their threat response within minutes when hearing the tone without the snake. But after over-activating sgACC, marmosets exhibited fearful behaviour and higher blood pressure for much longer. They also remained anxious around other types of threat (in the form of an unfamiliar human). This reaction showed they could no longer dampen down their threat responses. Being unable to regulate emotions is also seen in many patients with anxiety and depression.

These findings build on our earlier work that showed over-activity of sgACC reduces anticipation and motivation for rewards, mirroring the anhedonia (inability to feel pleasure) seen in depression. This suggests sgACC over-activity can cause two of the core symptoms seen in depression – negative emotions (including anxiety) and lack of pleasure.

## Heart disease and depression

Another outstanding question is why people with depression also have increased risk of heart disease. While there's undoubtedly lifestyle and socioeconomic factors linking heart disease and depression, we wanted to test whether sgACC over-activity itself could disrupt cardiovascular function. We thought this region might be important because it's connected to the brainstem, which regulates our heart rate and blood pressure.

We found that sgACC over-activity not only exaggerated marmosets' blood pressure response to threat, it also increased heart rate and reduced heart rate variability even at rest. Heart rate variability is an important measure of how rapidly the heart can adapt to changes in the environment, especially cues which predict reward or punishment.

These changes mirror some of the cardiac dysfunction seen in depression and anxiety. The elevated heart rate and reduced heart rate variability suggests that over-activity in sgACC promotes the body's 'fight-or-flight' response, which – if lasting over long periods of time – puts the heart under extra strain and might explain the increased incidence of heart disease.

## Treatment response

We also used brain imaging to investigate the other regions affected by sgACC over-activity in threatening situations. We saw increased activity in two key parts of the brain's stress network, the amygdala and hypothalamus. By contrast, reduced activity was seen in parts of the lateral prefrontal cortex, which regulates emotional responses and is underactive in depression. These changes were very different to those seen following over-activation during a rewarding situation.

Knowing these differences may be key to us understanding which treatments will be most effective depending on the symptoms exhibited by a patient. This then led us to investigate why some people respond to antidepressants while others don't. The most common type of antidepressants are selective serotonin re-uptake inhibitors (SSRIs). But up to one-third of people who take antidepressants are treatment resistant – meaning they don't respond to them. New treatments are urgently needed for these people.

Ketamine has shown some promise in successfully treating people with treatment resistant depression – and acts within hours to relieve symptoms. Previously, we had shown ketamine effectively treated anhedonia after sgACC had been over-activated.

But in our recent study, we found that ketamine could not improve the elevated anxiety-like responses the marmosets displayed towards the unfamiliar human. This shows us different depression and anxiety symptoms react differently to different types of antidepressants or treatments. On one hand, anhedonia was reversed by ketamine, while anxiety was not.

But over-activation of sgACC is likely to be just one underlying cause of depression and anxiety. Others may have altered activity in different regions of the prefrontal cortex, which are also linked to anxiety. There's still a long way to go before we have identified the different causes of depression and anxiety and which treatments can improve them. But our research shows that for some, targeting sgACC over-activity may be key in treating their symptoms.

*4 November 2020*

> **Research**
>
> Conduct some online research into the different types of antidepressant medications that are available on NHS prescription. Select one to look at in depth, considering its benefits and side effects, and share your findings with the rest of your group.

**THE CONVERSATION**

The above information is reprinted with kind permission from The Conversation.
© 2010-2023, The Conversation Trust (UK) Limited

www.theconversation.com

# Anxiety Triggers

Chapter 2

## COVID-19 pandemic triggers 25% increase in prevalence of anxiety and depression worldwide

Wake-up call to all countries to step up mental health services and support.

In the first year of the COVID-19 pandemic, global prevalence of anxiety and depression increased by a massive 25%, according to a scientific brief released by the World Health Organization (WHO) today. The brief also highlights who has been most affected and summarizes the effect of the pandemic on the availability of mental health services and how this has changed during the pandemic.

Concerns about potential increases in mental health conditions had already prompted 90% of countries surveyed to include mental health and psychosocial support in their COVID-19 response plans, but major gaps and concerns remain.

'The information we have now about the impact of COVID-19 on the world's mental health is just the tip of the iceberg,' said Dr Tedros Adhanom Ghebreyesus, WHO Director-General. 'This is a wake-up call to all countries to pay more attention to mental health and do a better job of supporting their populations' mental health.'

### Multiple stress factors

One major explanation for the increase is the unprecedented stress caused by the social isolation resulting from the pandemic. Linked to this were constraints on people's ability to work, seek support from loved ones and engage in their communities.

Loneliness, fear of infection, suffering and death for oneself and for loved ones, grief after bereavement and financial worries have also all been cited as stressors leading to anxiety and depression. Among health workers, exhaustion has been a major trigger for suicidal thinking.

### Young people and women worst hit

The brief, which is informed by a comprehensive review of existing evidence about the impact of COVID-19 on mental health and mental health services, and includes estimates from the latest Global Burden of Disease study, shows that the pandemic has affected the mental health of young people and that they are disproportionally at risk of suicidal and self-harming behaviours. It also indicates that women have been more severely impacted than men and that people with pre-existing physical health conditions, such as asthma, cancer and heart disease, were more likely to develop symptoms of mental disorders.

Data suggests that people with pre-existing mental disorders do not appear to be disproportionately vulnerable to COVID-19 infection. Yet, when these people do become infected, they are more likely to suffer hospitalization, severe illness and death compared with people without mental disorders. People with more severe mental disorders, such as psychoses, and young people with mental disorders, are particularly at risk.

### Gaps in care

This increase in the prevalence of mental health problems has coincided with severe disruptions to mental health services, leaving huge gaps in care for those who need it most. For much of the pandemic, services for mental, neurological and substance use conditions were the most disrupted among all essential health services reported by WHO Member States. Many countries also reported major disruptions in life-saving services for mental health, including for suicide prevention.

By the end of 2021 the situation had somewhat improved but today too many people remain unable to get the care and support they need for both pre-existing and newly developed mental health conditions.

Unable to access face-to-face care, many people have sought support online, signaling an urgent need to make reliable and effective digital tools available and easily accessible. However, developing and deploying digital interventions remains a major challenge in resource-limited countries and settings.

### WHO and country action

Since the early days of the pandemic, WHO and partners have worked to develop and disseminate resources in multiple languages and formats to help different groups cope with and respond to the mental health impacts of COVID-19. For example, WHO produced a story book for 6-11-year-olds, My Hero is You, now available in 142 languages and 61 multimedia adaptations, as well as a toolkit for supporting older adults available in 16 languages.

At the same time, the Organization has worked with partners, including other United Nations agencies, international nongovernmental organizations and the Red Cross and Red Crescent Societies, to lead an interagency mental health and psychosocial response to COVID-19. Throughout the pandemic, WHO has also worked to promote the integration of mental health and psychosocial support across and within all aspects of the global response.

WHO Member States have recognized the impact of COVID-19 on mental health and are taking action. WHO's most recent pulse survey on continuity of essential health services indicated that 90% of countries are working to provide mental health and psychosocial support to COVID-19 patients and responders alike. Moreover, at last year's World Health Assembly, countries emphasized the need to develop and strengthen mental health and psychosocial support services as part of strengthening preparedness, response and resilience to COVID-19 and future public health emergencies. They adopted the updated Comprehensive Mental Health Action Plan 2013-2030, which includes an indicator on preparedness for mental health and psychosocial support in public health emergencies.

### Step up investment

However, this commitment to mental health needs to be accompanied by a global step up in investment. Unfortunately, the situation underscores a chronic global shortage of mental health resources that continues today. WHO's most recent Mental Health Atlas showed that in 2020, governments worldwide spent on average just over 2% of their health budgets on mental health and many low-income countries reported having fewer than 1 mental health worker per 100 000 people.

Dévora Kestel, Director of the Department of Mental Health and Substance Use at WHO, sums up the situation: 'While the pandemic has generated interest in and concern for mental health, it has also revealed historical under-investment in mental health services. Countries must act urgently to ensure that mental health support is available to all.'

*2 March 2022*

The above information is reprinted with kind permission from the World Health Organization.
© 2023 WHO

www.who.int

# Young people around the world report high levels of climate anxiety

In the past few years, the effects of climate change have become undeniably apparent.

By Emma Barratt

In the last two years alone, headlines have been full of climate disasters – from forest fire smoke turning San Francisco's sky luminous red, to torrential flooding in Germany and China.

In the face of events like this, anxiety and fear about climate change is undoubtedly increasing. Far from being indicative of mental illness, climate anxiety (also known as eco-anxiety or climate distress) more neatly fits under the banner of 'practical anxiety': fear that motivates change to help us respond to threats. Even though this in itself is useful, the experiences of fear can be unrelenting, and have serious consequences for mental health and functioning.

Young people are more at risk than those from older generations; an uncertain and dangerous climate situation poses the most risk to their futures, after all.

It's with this in mind that Caroline Hickman and colleagues at the University of Bath set out to investigate the extent of young people's feelings and thoughts on climate change, and the functional impact associated with them. In their global study, posted as a preprint at SSRN, they look how the threats of climate change, as well as government response to these threats, affect the emotions and day to day functioning of young people.

Ten thousand participants aged between 16 and 25 years old were recruited via an online survey portal. These participants were based in ten different countries from around the world, as far flung as Australia, Brazil, India, and Finland. All completed a measure of climate anxiety constructed specifically for this study by 11 experts in relevant areas of psychology and law. Participants were not made aware of the topic of the survey before starting.

The measure itself contained eight broad sections; these related to worry about climate change, its impact on their functioning, emotions and thoughts about climate change, as well as feelings of being ignored on the topic, beliefs about government response to the threat, and the emotional impact of that response. In order to more closely investigate particular constructs, such as negative feelings about climate change or negative thoughts about government response, the team also condensed scores from relevant items across these sections during their analyses. And, last but not least, emotional impacts of government responses were split into two scales – the reassurance scale, and the betrayal scale – to allow closer analysis of positive and negative feelings, respectively.

Across all countries, the majority of participants (60%) reported feeling 'very' or 'extremely' worried about climate change. More than 45% reported that these feelings negatively impacted their daily lives. By country, those expressing the highest amount of worry tended to be from poorer regions, in the Global South, and those who had been more directly impacted by climate change. For example Portugal, where there have in recent years been extensive wildfires, rated highest for worry amongst its neighbours in the Global North.

Participants reported a wide range of negative emotions: 77% said the future was frightening, and over 50% had felt afraid, sad, anxious, angry, powerless, helpless, and/or guilty about climate change. Optimism and indifference, unfortunately, were not often reported. When talking to others about climate change, almost half of participants said their concerns had been ignored or dismissed.

When it came to rating government response, participants were generally unimpressed. Over 60% of respondents disagreed with every positive statement about their

government's climate action, though this did vary significantly between countries. Across all regions, however, feelings of betrayal were higher than those of reassurance.

Correlational analyses indicated close positive relationships between negative thoughts, worry about climate change, and impact on functioning. These factors also correlated strongly with feelings of government betrayal and negative beliefs about their response to the climate threats at hand, suggesting that those who believed the government to be underperforming in their response to climate change experienced more negative psychological consequences. In many, this is likely to constitute Moral Injury – significant psychological distress caused by witnessing a traumatic event that runs against the viewer's morals, that they are powerless to stop. Not only can Moral Injury further increase mental health risks, the authors say, but it could also open the door to lawsuits based on psychological harm.

The measure used in this study was not standardised, as no suitable measure existed previously, meaning further investigation as to its validity would likely be beneficial. And of course, the data is correlational, meaning that no conclusions about causality can be drawn from this data (no matter how intuitive they may feel).

Even so, taken together, the data collected in study stands as firm evidence that climate anxiety is evident across the globe. This continued stress on the younger members of our populations severely affects their emotions and ability to function day-to-day. Given the timescale of issues at hand, it's easy to imagine how the rapidly increasing threats of climate change could give rise to mental health issues among many young people, especially if governments continue to fail in their responses. Further research into these climate-specific stressors as precursors to mental health issues in young people will likely illuminate this relationship further.

The authors say that their results also demonstrate the point that climate anxiety isn't simply caused by ecological catastrophe: it's also directly related to government inaction. Greater levels of action and commitment by governments can not only enable us to limit warming to 1.5 degrees by the end of the century, it also has the potential to improve the mental wellbeing of citizens around the world.

*29 October 2021*

Emma L. Barratt (@E_Barratt) is a staff writer at BPS Research Digest

### Key Facts

- A global study by the University of Bath surveyed 10,000 young people aged 16-25 to collect their feelings about climate change.
- 60% of the participants reported feeling 'very' or 'extremely' worried about climate change.
- More than 45% reported these feelings negatively impacted their daily lives.

The above information is reprinted with kind permission from The British Psychological Society
© 2000-2023 The British Psychological Society

www.bps.org.uk

# Eco-anxiety is harming young people's mental health – but it doesn't have to

This article is part of: United Nations Climate Change Conference COP27

Dr. Katherine Grill, CEO & Cofounder, Neolth

- Climate change is fuelling a mental health 'eco-anxiety' crisis among our children and young people, some of it fuelled by social media and much by a feeling of powerlessness.
- 67% of Americans aged 18 to 23 are somewhat to very concerned about the impact of climate change on their mental health.
- But this can be combated by taking meaningful action, such as campaigning or volunteering, that gives children a sense of agency and control.

During the COVID-19 pandemic, the communities worldwide experienced sharp increases in stress, anxiety, depression and suicidality. Systemic shortcomings in access to mental health services emerged, with billions in funding allocated to improved solutions.

But those solutions need to be supported by an in-depth understanding of how certain factors impact mental health – not least, climate change.

The connection of hurricanes, wildfires and floods to physical health is clear: they cause injury, hospitalization and death and damage the infrastructure used to provide food, water, sewage, technology and medical supplies.

What is less well-understood is the impact of extreme weather events on mental health – especially when it comes to children.

## Trauma, mental health and extreme weather events

Trauma and shock can occur after witnessing injuries or deaths of loved ones, or damage to personal property or the loss of livelihood, such as the destruction of small businesses. Studies of adult survivors indicate a prevalence of PTSD between 30-60% in the first year following a disaster event. Even if PTSD does not develop, survivors are at risk of anxiety or depression.

Historically, extreme weather events were seen as one-time natural disasters where survivors could recover and rebuild. With the acceleration of climate change, communities are experiencing recurring disaster events from which it is difficult to recover.

As extreme weather events increase in occurrence, the public becomes more aware of climate change. According to the American Psychological Association, 75% of Americans are concerned about climate change and 25% are alarmed – a figure that has doubled since 2017.

The worsening of climate change and growing awareness of it mean that it's no longer just survivors who are experiencing mental health effects. Initially documented in 2007, a new phenomenon is emerging called eco-anxiety.

## Eco-anxiety – a driver of the mental health pandemic

Eco-anxiety is worry about the future that can result in fear, anger, powerlessness, exhaustion, stress or sadness. While there has been debate in the medical community about the exact definition, there is consensus that uncertainty and uncontrollability fuel eco-anxiety.

And eco-anxiety is more prevalent among young people.

This might be because young people have a more uncertain future, and thus view climate change as more of a threat than older generations. Other factors play a role too: identifying as female, not being able to take action and having a strong connection to the land can make eco-anxiety worse.

Social media, too, plays a role. People, especially children, are now learning about climate change through social media. Witnessing natural disasters online, while different from living through them, can catalyze the development of eco-anxiety. Adults can reassure children by engaging in behavior that actively combats climate change. Protective factors against eco-anxiety include participating in activism, trusting in technology and developing a sense of agency over climate change.

### A risk to our children and economy

As billions in funding is directed towards mental health following the COVID-19 pandemic, it is important that proposed solutions encompass burgeoning issues like eco-anxiety. Otherwise, we risk spending on solutions that don't address the full spectrum of mental health concerns.

This is especially important in the field of youth mental health, where recipients of care have a heightened awareness of the intersectionality between these fields: 67% of Americans aged 18 to 23 are somewhat to very concerned about the impact of climate change on their mental health.

When developing mental health solutions that address eco-anxiety, including for the youth, solutions providers should consider various types of coping behaviors and their associated outcomes, including:

**Problem-focused coping**: making active strides to address climate change.

**Emotion-focused coping:** managing negative emotions related to climate change.

**Meaning-focused coping:** managing negative emotions related to climate change, while simultaneously promoting positive emotions like hope by combating climate change.

While emotion-focused coping has been the most common strategy used by adolescents and young adults to date, research has found that meaning-focused coping is the most effective in regards to eco-anxiety. When done correctly, meaning-focused coping, such as getting involved in the fight against climate change through volunteering or campaigning, facilitates positive emotions like hope without ignoring negative ones like anger or anxiety.

The end result is processing, rather than getting stuck in, anxiety and feeling motivated to engage in activism and other pro-environmental behavior.

Not only will this improve the mental health of those worrying about climate change, but it will also contribute to the grassroots movement to protect our planet.

*1 November 2022*

The views expressed in this article are those of the author alone and not the World Economic Forum.

The above information is reprinted with kind permission from World Economic Forum
© 2023 World Economic Forum

www.weforum.org

# Stress, anxiety and hopelessness over personal finances widespread across UK – new mental health survey

A poll finds one in ten (10%) of UK adults feeling hopeless about financial circumstances, more than one-third (34%) feeling anxious, and almost three in ten (29%) feeling stressed in the past month.

The Mental Health Foundation asks for government action on supporting people at higher risk and preventing mental health problems ahead of the Autumn Statement.

Foundation warns of a significant rise in mental health problems without adequate support.

The UK population is experiencing widespread levels of stress, anxiety and hopelessness in response to financial concerns, according to a new survey commissioned by the Mental Health Foundation.

Ahead of the Chancellor's autumn statement, the Foundation warns that action needs to be taken to prevent a significant rise in mental health problems across the UK, as large numbers of people report feeling anxious, hopeless or stressed due to their financial circumstances.

The survey of 3000 adults aged 18 and over, conducted by Opinium between 7 to 14 November 2022, found that 29% of adults experienced stress, 34% experienced anxiety and 10% said they felt hopeless because of financial worries during the previous month.

When thinking about the next few months, UK adults are most concerned about not being able to maintain their standard of living (71%), heat their home (66%) or pay general monthly household bills (61%). Significantly, half (50%) of UK adults were at least a little worried about being able to afford food over the next few months, rising to 67% of younger adults aged 18 to 34.

The Foundation is calling on the UK Government to ensure people across the UK will be protected from the negative impact of both the cost of living crisis and potential cuts to public services.

This includes protecting financial benefits, so they rise with inflation, and increasing the capacity of debt services, food banks, community organisations and social security departments. It also includes training staff on addressing the trauma many claimants have experienced.

Evidence has repeatedly shown that financial strain and poverty are key contributors to mental health problems. The Foundation warns that the number of people experiencing poor mental health will likely increase rapidly as more people struggle to make ends meet.

Mark Rowland, Chief Executive of Mental Health Foundation, said:

*'Our findings are a warning sign of the mental health consequences of the cost of living crisis. We must protect public services and benefits at this crucial time. If people are struggling to meet their essential needs for a warm home and enough healthy food for their families, we can expect a significant rise in mental health problems as the burden of financial strain continues to take its toll.*

*The challenge the country faces cannot be easily addressed. However, there are steps we can take to protect people's mental health at this time. We must support those at higher risk by, for example, raising benefits in line with inflation and employers committing to pay their staff the real living wage. Training frontline staff in social security and debt services on how to recognise and respond sensitively to the trauma experienced by many people they are working with can also help.*

*Preventing mental health problems is vital. Our mental health services are already stretched beyond capacity; we cannot sit on the sidelines and watch them collapse under ever-greater demand.*

*The UK Government should consider the mental health impact of all decisions that affect the cost of living crisis. Other measures we ask for include maintaining and extending free or subsidised public transport to allow people to connect with friends and family and increasing the provision of debt advice and other vital community services.'*

Earlier this year, the Foundation published research with the London School of Economics and Political Science, which put the cost of mental health problems to the UK economy at £117 billion annually.

While the Mental Health Foundation is calling on political leaders to take action, it has also published guidance for people experiencing financial strain. This includes signposting to support services.

*17 November 2022*

### Activity

Research some support service and charities in your local area that can help people with concerns over their personal finances. Create a signposting poster or leaflet for those services.

The above information is reprinted with kind permission from Mental Health Foundation
© 2023 All Rights Reserved

www.mentalhealth.org.uk

# What's driving the female anxiety epidemic?

Holly Fisher was 37 when her anxiety finally reached a crisis point – but it was a moment that had been building since childhood. Playground bullying faded into body image issues, which paved the way for 'quite major' social anxiety that dominated her adult life.

At my worst, I have had full-blown panic attacks where I felt like I couldn't breathe. My heart was racing and I felt like I was going to faint', she recalled.

'The strange thing is that everyone thinks I'm incredibly outgoing and confident so it's come as quite a shock to my family, who I hid it from'.

Holly's only respite was alcohol, which provided a confidence boost when nothing else could calm her – but it came at a cost.

'My mind would come up with a million excuses why I shouldn't go out', she said, opening up about her experiences to raise awareness.

'Ironically I gave up drinking because my anxiety got totally out of control – especially hangxiety', she says. Hangovers would leave her with sweaty palms, a quickened heart rate and a stutter.

But Holly's experiences weren't always clear, even to herself. 'I didn't realise it was anxiety when I was younger', she explained. 'It probably started up really badly in my early twenties. I bounced in and out of sobriety for many years because of my anxiety'.

Tales like these are surprisingly common. Hospital admissions for anxiety have soared since 2017 and the condition affects women the most.

The NHS defines anxiety as a 'feeling of unease, such as worry or fear, that can be mild or severe'. This sense of dread seeps into many aspects of women's lives. In fact, a recent study from the online will makers at Beyond found women are even twice as anxious about death compared to men.

So, what's behind this trend? We spoke to Antonella Santuccione-Chadha, co-founder and CEO of the Women's Brain Project, about the statistics.

She thinks the ways mental health conditions are researched 'are biased' – and wants to see treatments and prevention policies tailored to women.

'The brain is an organ like any other', says Antonella. 'The scientific community is learning day by day that this is the case'.

Her organisation seeks to highlight the many brain-related conditions that affect women more, including anxiety disorders, Alzheimer's disease and stroke. The aim is to create a global research institute focused on women.

Antonella thinks the statistics on women's anxiety are partly explained by social factors.

'The role of the woman within our society could make us more prone to feeling anxious, given the performance we are expected to deliver', she surmises.

'Anxiety can be a symptom of other diseases, too. Anxiety could be the way something else manifests in a woman.

'Or it could just be anxiety because of the way we live our lives, and the pressures we have from society'.

But, she wants to stress how these social differences – such as the care burden, which sees women taking on as much as 60 per cent more unpaid work than men – can shape us physically.

'The brain is very receptive to any type of influence that we receive from outside, more than any other organ', she says, noting that trauma can change the brain.

'Caring roles, or being a mother, might result in sleep deprivation and these are the kinds of things which can pose a higher risk for brain health'.

Antonella is leading the fight-back by pushing for better research, which she hopes will aid precision treatments and preventative measures for women. She maintains: 'It's about asking: what would be useful for this group of people? The general approach is resulting in a huge waste of money'.

Antonella believes digitisation of psychiatry represents an opportunity – providing it is done properly.

'If a data set is not representative it won't be helpful', she argues. Current medical research often excludes female participants – at its worst, this practice means women are denied life-saving HIV drugs.

The failure to effectively tailor research could be one reason why anxiety remains so prevalent among women, despite the range of treatments now available. But, for now, we'll need to wait for the science to catch up.

'The main problem I see is that we should understand the differences between men and women', concludes Antonella.

For Holly, things had to reach rock bottom before they got better. The 'watershed moment' came when she suffered a miscarriage in 2017. The Brightonian then sought therapy and used self-care techniques, including 'tapping, mindfulness, meditation, fresh air and gentle exercise', to aid her recovery.

'You name it, I've tried it!' she says.

The 39-year-old now runs the Instagram account Sobersista, where she documents her recovery and speaks out about mental health. She is also an HR consultant with her own business – and has just become a mother.

'I think my attitude toward anxiety is improving because I feel more positive about myself', she says, adding that motherhood has given her a new confidence to work on her own terms.

'I'm doing me', she says.

*7 January 2020*

The above information is reprinted with kind permission from SOUK
© 2023 Shout Out Uk. All rights reserved

www.shoutoutuk.org

# Phone call anxiety: why so many of us have it, and how to get over it

An article from The Conversation.

By Ilham Sebah, Teaching Fellow in Psychology, Royal Holloway, University of London

Staying in touch with loved ones without seeing them in person has become even more important during the pandemic. But for some people, making or receiving calls is a stressful experience. Phone anxiety – or telephobia – is the fear and avoidance of phone conversations and it's common among those with social anxiety disorder.

Having a hatred of your phone doesn't necessarily mean you have phone anxiety, although the two can be related. There are, of course, many people who dislike making or receiving calls. But if this dislike causes you to experience certain symptoms, you may have phone anxiety.

Some emotional symptoms of phone anxiety include delaying or avoiding making calls because of heightened anxiety, feeling extremely nervous or anxious before, during and after the call and obsessing or worrying about what you'll say. Physical symptoms include nausea, increase in heart rate, shortness of breath, dizziness and muscular tension.

If you feel like this, you're not alone. A 2019 survey of UK office workers found 76% of millennials and 40% of baby boomers have anxious thoughts when their phone rings. Because of this, 61% of millennials would completely avoid calls, compared with 42% of baby boomers. If you suffer from these symptoms, there are some things you can do to make it easier.

## Avoiding phone calls

Talking on the phone can be daunting because we're limited to just the sounds of our voices. In the absence of all other social cues – including gestures, body language and eye contact – we can often feel self-conscious of the sound of our own voices and our choice of words.

Thanks to technology, we can often go days, weeks or even months without directly speaking to others on the phone. One study found anxious people prefer texting over phone calls, rating it a superior medium for expressive and intimate contact.

Some people opt for texting because it gives them time to think about the wording of their messages, providing the opportunity to be informal. In some cases, they develop a different personality separate and in contrast to their real-life, more reticent, self.

Research also suggests phone anxiety is related to a preoccupation with what the other person thinks of them. By eliminating the immediate reaction of others in spoken conversations, text messaging may offer those with phone anxiety a way of making social contact without the fear of rejection or disapproval.

Another reason phone calls can sometimes feel overwhelming is the pressure that comes with being someone else's focus. In face-to-face conversations, we have several distractions in our environment; like gazing out of the window or, ironically, checking the missed call notifications on our phones. This can make the interaction feel more casual and the conversation flow naturally. On a call, there are no external distractions, so it can feel like the spotlight is on us to answer questions straight away.

Pauses can feel extremely uncomfortable too. In person, you can see when someone is distracted or thinking but on the phone brief silences can feel awkward. We're also becoming accustomed to being able to review emails, texts and social media posts before hitting the send button, so a phone conversation can feel impulsive and risky.

It's easy to put off or completely avoid calls when you're feeling anxious, but the more you procrastinate, the worse the anxiety is likely to get. The good news is you don't need to suffer in silence, or over text messages. There are several useful techniques that may help you break the pattern.

## Pick up the phone

One of the most effective ways to overcome phone anxiety is to expose yourself to more phone calls. The more you do it, the less overwhelming it becomes. It's also likely that your phone anxiety is linked to a lack of experience. The more practice you have, the less anxious and more confident you'll feel.

You can start this process by making a list of the people you need to speak to on the phone, such as friends or colleagues, and go through each one by reflecting on what it is about the call that makes you anxious. For example, it might be making a mistake or feeling judged. When the call is over, acknowledging your success will help you stay motivated for the next call.

If you've tried to combat your phone anxiety or you think you might benefit from seeking professional help, counselling is a great option and there are a number of talking therapies available. Cognitive behavioural therapy is a very effective treatment for social anxiety, and there's an online option that might be a suitable alternative if you feel a bit nervous about speaking to someone in person.

*23 February 2021*

THE CONVERSATION

The above information is reprinted with kind permission from The Conversation.
© 2010-2023, The Conversation Trust (UK) Limited

www.theconversation.com

# Why the root of your anxiety might not be your mind

With so many people struggling in so many ways, one author believes it is more than just mental wiring or genetics to blame.

By Rosa Silverman

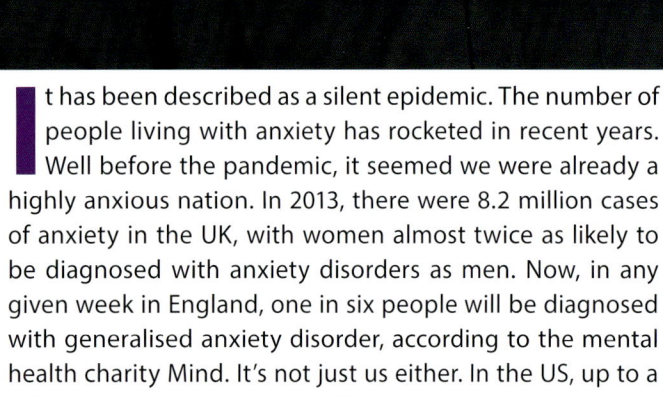

It has been described as a silent epidemic. The number of people living with anxiety has rocketed in recent years. Well before the pandemic, it seemed we were already a highly anxious nation. In 2013, there were 8.2 million cases of anxiety in the UK, with women almost twice as likely to be diagnosed with anxiety disorders as men. Now, in any given week in England, one in six people will be diagnosed with generalised anxiety disorder, according to the mental health charity Mind. It's not just us either. In the US, up to a third of people are said to be affected by an anxiety disorder in their lifetime.

The numbers are so enormous, they can seem hard to credit. But Dr Ellen Vora, an American psychiatrist and author of a new book, The Anatomy of Anxiety, has an explanation – and it lies not in our mental wiring or genetics, but instead in our bodies. Essentially, in what we are putting into them and how we are looking after them.

It may be an unsettling thought, but what if instead of suffering from an anxiety disorder, for which the only effective remedy was medication, you were actually drinking too much caffeine? Or failing to regulate your blood sugar, get enough sleep or place sufficient boundaries between your work and home life?

These variables may sound too simple to explain the feelings of uncontrollable worry, fear or unease that plague the lives of those with anxiety. But, says Vora, they really are the root cause far more often than we might think.

This is more than just a theory: she has seen not only her patients' mental health issues resolve after they have made some basic physical changes, but also her own.

'I do think we've fundamentally misunderstood mental health,' says New York-based Vora when we speak over Zoom. From being shrouded in 'shame and secrecy', mental illness has evolved to being seen as a chemical imbalance, she says. 'It's taken away that moral judgment and people really take comfort in the idea that "it's my genes, it's my brain chemistry", [they] really like that idea and it came with this promise of "it's your serotonin and therefore take this pill and you will feel better".'

Except there is a 'but'. Vora is not opposed to medication per se; she's aware it works for some. But for others, it demonstrably doesn't. Not only this, but it can produce what she calls 'negative downstream effects', such as problems coming off the pills once you are on them.

'I want to know the true root cause [of the anxiety], identify it and address it and then obviate the need for medication,' says Vora, who takes a functional medicine approach to mental health, considering the whole person rather than focusing on a specific symptom in isolation.

The good news is the true root cause is quite often something we can tackle: a physical trigger that activates a stress response in our body, which, Vora writes 'transmits signals up to our brain telling us something is not right and our brain, in turn, offers a narrative for why we feel uneasy'.

But the real reason we feel uneasy, she argues, is a state of physiological imbalance in the body: 'Something as simple as a blood sugar crash or a bout of gut inflammation.'

What we're experiencing, in this scenario, is what Vora calls false anxiety: our modern diet and habits, or the constant stream of information and messages we're receiving through multiple channels, can initiate the kind of stress response our ancestors might have experienced when facing a threatening wild animal. Tweak our diet and habits and we can dampen down this response and thus our anxiety, she believes.

She acknowledges her thinking runs counter to the modern reflex among overstretched doctors to either prescribe medication to suppress anxiety symptoms or refer the patient to an interminable waiting list for overstretched mental health services. But she knows from experience how effective her alternative approach can be.

She was in her early 20s and a medical student at Columbia University when she herself became 'out of balance and really unwell in a number of different ways'. She was suffering everything from depression and disordered eating to irregular periods, migraines, acne and joint pain, and 'kept getting sicker'.

Undeterred by her advisers' scepticism, she studied to be a yoga teacher, trained in functional and integrated medicine, learned about nutrition and stopped eating gluten, which it turned out she had an intolerance to. 'What I learned directly in my own body was every holistic intervention I tried far outclassed any of the pharmaceutical interventions I did,' she says. 'That was what actually got me well. Then I started to experiment with this with patients.'

One of her early patients, who was keen to try an alternative to medication, was a woman with severe anxiety, depression and a history of trauma. Vora suggested some dietary changes: cutting out processed foods and cooking herself simple and healthy whole foods instead.

'It really turned her life completely around and she was off all medications by the end,' says Vora.

Not everyone is equally receptive to the idea that their anxiety originates in their body rather than their mind. 'I have patients for whom it's been utterly transformative, it's been life-changing. They were having frequent panic attacks and now they don't,' says Vora. '[But] I've noticed a lot of us initially bristle when we're feeling anxious and we connect with that feeling, we identify with it and it becomes our subjective reality and all these justifications the brain brings in feel very true and convincing, so if I come along and say "no it's actually just that you had an extra-strong coffee today", it can feel invalidating.'

She aims not to invalidate her patients' feelings, but to show them that 'we can probably feel a bit less anxious just by addressing these physical causes'.

And she wants her approach to be seen not as placing blame on individuals for their mental illness, but as a 'hopeful and empowering message [that] it's not your destiny, there is something we can do to change the outcome'.

Some diet and lifestyle tweaks are easier to make than others, of course. Anyone can tell us we shouldn't stress out about work; it's harder to put that into practice.

'I don't think I have the perfect solution but there are a lot of strategies that can at least help, and short of overturning our capitalist society and changing the way corporations value time and wellbeing, there's a lot of room around addressing our own perfectionism,' says Vora. 'We have to be very proactive about boundaries. [For] so many of us our jobs aren't confined to the work day. That blurred boundary [resulting from knowledge economy workers' ability to do their jobs from anywhere now] means there's nowhere that's protected and purely a place for leisure.'

She encourages her patients to put boundaries firmly in place; to institute a ritual before they start working and at the end of the day to help their brain transition between work and leisure. And she promotes a mantra of 'all I can do is do my reasonable best and that's enough'.

It's tougher to stick to than it sounds. But Vora is optimistic that those who adopt it can help change our stress and anxiety – inducing workplace culture from within.

'I've noticed a lot of us carry a fear that if we set boundaries with work we'll be perceived as lazy or unmotivated and might lose our job. What I've noticed with my patients is as they start to impose healthy boundaries around work, like not responding to a work email late at night or on a weekend, rather than being seen as lazy they actually start to train people to have more reasonable expectations of them,' she says. 'So it ends up becoming a virtuous circle.'

Vora makes the distinction between the false anxiety described above and what she calls true anxiety. 'False anxiety is the body communicating that there is a physiological imbalance, usually through a stress response, whereas true anxiety is the body communicating an essential message about our lives,' she writes.

It is existential anxiety, 'This is what it means to be human – to know the inherent vulnerability of walking this earth, that we can lose the people we love and that we, too, will one day die.'

But true anxiety can actually help keep us safe. It can prompt us to 'protect ourselves and keep our lives in motion,' she suggests.

Vora tells her patients that while rooting out the physical causes of their false anxiety, they should embrace their true anxiety and listen to what it is telling them. Because in her view, what it's telling them is that the world needs to change. 'It is critical that we shift from pathologising and suppressing this anxiety to heeding its urgent messages,' she writes. 'We need to listen to those with their ears to the ground, who sense the subtle – and not so subtle – dangers on the horizon. They are our prophets, and they may just wake us all up in time.'

*15 March 2022*

### Write

Write a list of boundaries that you can put in place to have a healthy working life.

Plan a before- and after-work (or school) ritual to help you transition between work and relaxation.

The above information is reprinted with kind permission from *The Telegraph*.
© Telegraph Media Group Limited 2022

**www.telegraph.co.uk**

# Chapter 3: Managing Anxiety

## Treatment – generalised anxiety disorder in adults

Generalised anxiety disorder (GAD) is a long-term condition, but a number of different treatments can help.

### Psychological therapies for GAD

If you have been diagnosed with GAD, you'll usually be advised to try psychological treatment before you're prescribed medication.

You can get talking therapies like cognitive behavioural therapy (CBT) and applied relaxation on the NHS.

You can refer yourself directly to an NHS talking therapies service without a referral from a GP.

Or your GP can refer you if you prefer.

### Guided self-help and cognitive behavioural therapy (CBT)

Your GP or talking therapies service may suggest trying a self-help course to see if it can help you learn to cope with your anxiety.

Self-help courses for GAD are usually based on the principles of cognitive behavioural therapy (CBT).

CBT is a type of talking therapy that can help you manage your problems by changing the way you think and behave.

CBT is one of the most effective treatments for GAD.

There are several ways you may be offered self-help and CBT:

- you work through a CBT workbook or computer course in your own time
- you work through a CBT workbook or computer course with the support of a therapist who you see every 1 or 2 weeks
- you take part in a group course where you and other people with similar problems meet with a therapist every week to learn ways to tackle your anxiety

If these initial treatments don't help, you'll usually be offered more intensive CBT where you usually have weekly sessions with a therapist for 3 to 4 months, or another type of therapy called applied relaxation or medication.

You can try some self-help cognitive behavioural therapy (CBT) techniques on the Every Mind Matters website. This is not a full CBT course or guided self-help, but it has practical self-help tips and strategies based on CBT techniques.

### Applied relaxation

Applied relaxation focuses on relaxing your muscles in a particular way during situations that usually cause anxiety.

The technique needs to be taught by a trained therapist and generally involves:

- learning how to relax your muscles
- learning how to relax your muscles quickly and in response to a trigger, such as the word 'relax'
- practising relaxing your muscles in situations that make you anxious

As with CBT, applied relaxation therapy will usually mean meeting with a therapist for a 1-hour session every week for 3 to 4 months.

Relaxation therapy may not be available in all areas, so you might be offered CBT instead.

### Medication

If the psychological treatments above haven't helped or you'd prefer not to try them, you'll usually be offered medication.

Your GP can prescribe a variety of different types of medication to treat GAD.

Some medication is designed to be taken on a short-term basis, while others are prescribed for longer periods.

Depending on your symptoms, you may need medication to treat your physical symptoms, as well as your psychological ones.

If you're considering taking medication for GAD, your GP should discuss the different options with you in detail before you start a course of treatment, including:

- the different types of medication
- length of treatment
- side effects and possible interactions with other medicines
- which medication is best for you if you're pregnant, planning a pregnancy or breastfeeding

You should also have regular appointments with your doctor to assess your progress when you're taking medication for GAD.

These will usually take place every 2 to 4 weeks for the first 3 months, then every 3 months after that.

Tell your GP if you think you may be experiencing side effects from your medication. They may be able to adjust your dose or prescribe an alternative medication.

### Selective serotonin reuptake inhibitors (SSRIs)

In most cases, the first medication you'll be offered will be a type of antidepressant called a selective serotonin reuptake inhibitor (SSRI).

This type of medication works by increasing the level of a chemical called serotonin in your brain.

Examples of SSRIs you may be prescribed include:

- sertraline
- escitalopram
- paroxetine

SSRIs can be taken on a long-term basis but, as with all antidepressants, they can take several weeks to start working.

You'll usually be started on a low dose, which may be gradually increased as your body adjusts to the medication.

Common side effects of SSRIs include:

- feeling agitated
- feeling or being sick
- indigestion
- diarrhoea or constipation
- loss of appetite and weight loss
- dizziness
- blurred vision
- dry mouth
- excessive sweating
- headaches
- problems sleeping (insomnia) or drowsiness
- low sex drive
- difficulty achieving orgasm during sex or masturbation
- in men, difficulty obtaining or maintaining an erection (erectile dysfunction)

These side effects should improve over time, although some may be related to your underlying condition.

### Serotonin and noradrenaline reuptake inhibitors (SNRIs)

If SSRIs don't help ease your anxiety, you may be prescribed a different type of antidepressant known as a serotonin and noradrenaline reuptake inhibitor (SNRI).

This type of medication increases the amount of serotonin and noradrenaline in your brain.

Examples of SNRIs you may be prescribed include:

- venlafaxine
- duloxetine

Common side effects of SNRIs include:

- feeling sick
- headaches
- drowsiness
- dizziness
- dry mouth
- constipation
- insomnia
- sweating
- sexual problems, such as low sex drive or difficulty getting an erection

SNRIs can also increase your blood pressure, so your blood pressure will be monitored regularly during treatment.

As with SSRIs, some of the side effects (such as feeling sick, an upset stomach, problems sleeping and feeling agitated or more anxious) are more common in the first 1 or 2 weeks of treatment, but these usually settle as your body adjusts to the medication.

### Stopping antidepressants

If your medication is not helping after about 2 months of treatment or it's causing unpleasant side effects, your GP may prescribe an alternative medication.

When you and your GP decide it's appropriate for you to stop taking your medication, you'll normally have your dose slowly reduced over the course of a few weeks to reduce the risk of withdrawal effects.

Never stop taking your medication unless your GP specifically advises you to.

### Pregabalin

If SSRIs and SNRIs aren't suitable for you, you may be offered pregabalin.

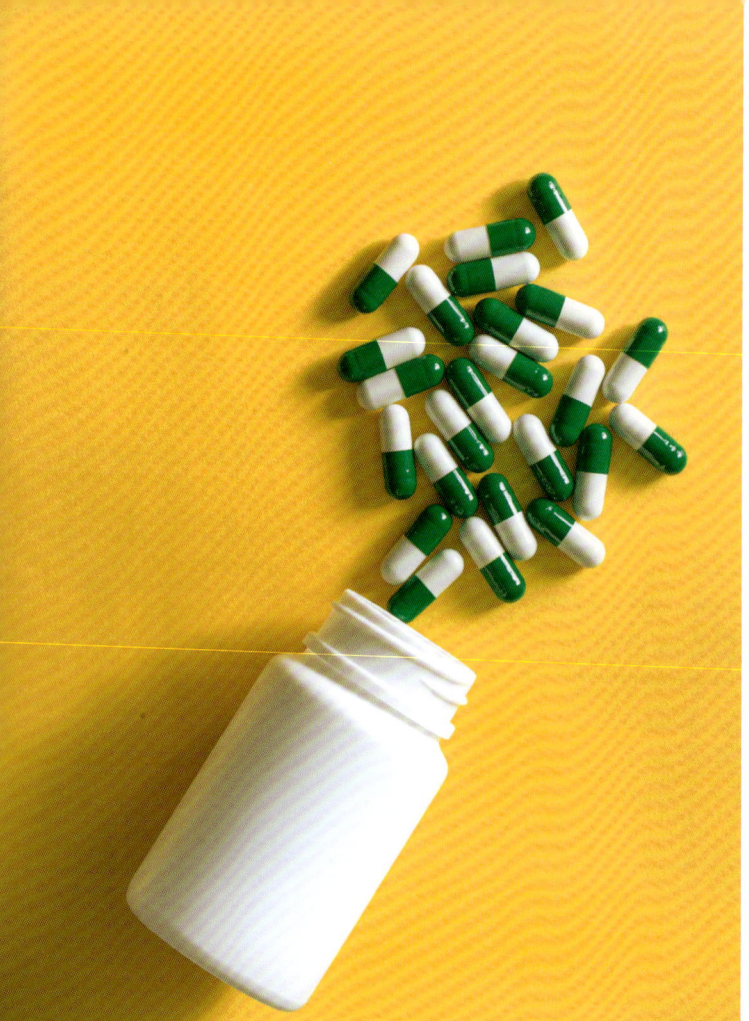

This is a medication known as an anticonvulsant, which is used to treat conditions such as epilepsy, but it's also been found to be beneficial in treating anxiety.

Side effects of pregabalin can include:

- drowsiness
- dizziness
- increased appetite and weight gain
- blurred vision
- headaches
- dry mouth
- vertigo

## Benzodiazepines

Benzodiazepines are a type of sedative that may sometimes be used as a short-term treatment during a particularly severe period of anxiety.

This is because they help ease the symptoms within 30 to 90 minutes of taking the medication.

If you're prescribed a benzodiazepine, it'll usually be diazepam.

Although benzodiazepines are very effective in treating the symptoms of anxiety, they can't be used for long periods.

This is because they can become addictive if used for longer than 4 weeks. Benzodiazepines also start to lose their effectiveness after this time.

For these reasons, you won't usually be prescribed benzodiazepines for any longer than 2 to 4 weeks at a time.

Side effects of benzodiazepines can include:

- drowsiness
- difficulty concentrating
- headaches
- vertigo
- an uncontrollable shake or tremble in part of the body (tremor)
- low sex drive

As drowsiness is a particularly common side effect of benzodiazepines, your ability to drive or operate machinery may be affected by taking this medication.

You should avoid these activities during treatment.

You should also never drink alcohol or use opiate drugs when taking benzodiazepine as doing so can be dangerous.

## Referral to a specialist

If you have tried the treatments mentioned above and have significant symptoms of GAD, you may want to discuss with your GP whether you should be referred to a mental health specialist.

A referral will work differently in different areas of the UK, but you'll usually be referred to your community mental health team.

These teams include a range of specialists, including:

- psychiatrists
- psychiatric nurses
- clinical psychologists
- occupational therapists
- social workers

An appropriate mental health specialist from your local team will carry out an overall reassessment of your condition.

They'll ask you about your previous treatment and how effective you found it.

They may also ask about things in your life that may be affecting your condition, or how much support you get from family and friends.

Your specialist will then be able to devise a treatment plan for you, which will aim to treat your symptoms.

As part of this plan, you may be offered a treatment you haven't tried before, which might be psychological treatments or medication.

Alternatively, you may be offered a combination of a psychological treatment with a medication, or a combination of 2 different medications.

*5 October 2022*

The above information is reprinted with kind permission from the NHS.
© Crown Copyright 2023
This information is licensed under the Open Government Licence v3.0
To view this licence, visit http://www.nationalarchives.gov.uk/doc/open-government-licence/

www.nhs.uk

# Tips to look after your mental health during scary world events

Scary world news can affect our mental health. After learning about global events that cause uncertainty, you may feel fear, anxiety or a loss of control over your own life and plans. You may worry for the safety of strangers, loved ones or yourself. And if you have lived through similar events in the past, it may bring up traumatic memories.

Know that whatever you feel is valid. Know that we care about you and your mental health. And know that you are not alone in this.

We have created some advice to help you cope and support your loved ones during these uncertain times.

## Stay informed, but be aware of your limits

Ask yourself, 'how much information and scary world news am I currently taking in? And how does it make me feel?'

If it's having a negative effect on how you feel, try to:

- take a short break from the news
- mute or turn off news notifications on your smartphone
- mute or unfollow social media accounts that are reporting on it
- or limit your news intake to once a day

After you've had a break, ask yourself 'how do I feel now that I've had a space from the news?'

If you find that the break has helped, then try to continue:

- to stay informed in bitesize portions
- to take space from the news when you need to
- to pause and check in on how you feel
- to engage with different social media platforms based on how they make you feel

Over and above those, try to be intentional in how you are consuming news, and, as much as you can, avoid long 'scrolling through' sessions.

Try to accept that, although we may want to help or change the current global and national situation, some of these things may be out of our control.

We talk about ways that you can meaningfully engage or feel empowered in the sections below.

## Engage with your community in a meaningful way

If the uncertainty surrounding the news is bringing about feelings of fear and isolation, remember that there are always other people that are feeling the exact same way right now and that there are things that we can do to tackle this.

issues: Anxiety — Chapter 3: Managing Anxiety

Something you can do to tackle these feelings is to connect with your local community. This can help you to feel more empowered, connected and less alone.

Connect with your local community by:

- getting involved in local volunteering opportunities
- joining local grassroots campaigns, or community groups working on issues that are important to you
- joining a local Facebook group or Meet Ups to connect with people in your local area

Humans are neurologically wired to connect with others. Helping others and engaging with our local community in a meaningful way is good for our mental health.

### Empower your voice

You may feel powerless if you have opinions on what is happening in the world but remain silent. And you may feel powerless if you don't know what to do with your opinions or passion for change.

Here are some ways that you can empower your voice and feel less out of control:

- explore ways to be engaged in a political community
- take part in a peaceful organised rally
- join relevant events or debates.

Civic and political activism may make you feel more empowered and give you an avenue to express your thoughts in a constructive way.

When talking to other people about world news, if a topic comes up which you disagree on, try to focus on active listening, respectful discussion and assertive communication. Being drawn into highly polarised or disrespectful conversations usually has an adverse effect on our wellbeing.

If a comment upsets you, try to take a break, pause the conversation and come back when you feel ready.

### Don't bottle it up

When you feel overwhelmed, try to reach out for support. There are people and organisations that want to help:

- talk to a friend, family member or your GP
- call a helpline: call Samaritans on 116 123 (UK)
- join Mind's online community:
- join Side by Side
- message a text support line: text SHOUT to 85258 (UK)

You could also try to express how you are feeling through creativity. You could write in a journal, listen to an emotive song, draw or dance. Express in a way that feels right for you. Try to stay with those activities for at least a few minutes to unlock their protective effects on your wellbeing.

### Look after your mental health

Try to keep allocating time to things, activities and actions that are good for your mental health.

What works will be different for each person, so tune into what is right for you. Here are a few things to get your started. Try to:

- have a healthy sleep routine: check out our top tips for good sleep
- bring movement into your day: check out our tips for looking after your mental health with exercise
- nourish your body and mind with healthy foods: check out our information on diet and mental health
- spend quality time with friends, family and loved ones
- connect with nature to help reduce stress and improve your mood

All of these can help you to feel better and to take your mind off the stress of the news cycle.

Finally, if you feel that scary world news is affecting your children, then use our guide to talking to your children about scary world news to help you have open and honest conversations at home.

*2022*

### Research

In pairs, do some research online and find three positive 'good news' stories to share with the rest of your class.

The above information is reprinted with kind permission from Mental Health Foundation.
© 2023 Mental Health Foundation

www.mentalhealth.org.uk

# 4 relaxation techniques to combat stress and anxiety

### Life can be really busy.

Whether you're doing school work, socialising with friends or playing sport, sometimes it can be easy to forget to take some time out just for yourself.

If you don't give yourself have time to relax, you might start to feel:

- stressed
- no longer in control of your life or that you're rushing from one thing to the next • anxious
- overwhelmed

Relaxation can be a great way to relieve stress, worry and anxiety.

If you're finding it difficult to cope then support is available, reach out to a trusted adult or your school nurse.

### Breathing exercises

Breathing exercises can take just a few minutes and can be done anywhere as a quick time out, whether you're standing, sitting or lying down. But you'll get the most benefit if you practise them on a daily basis.

Here's a short exercise you can try anytime:

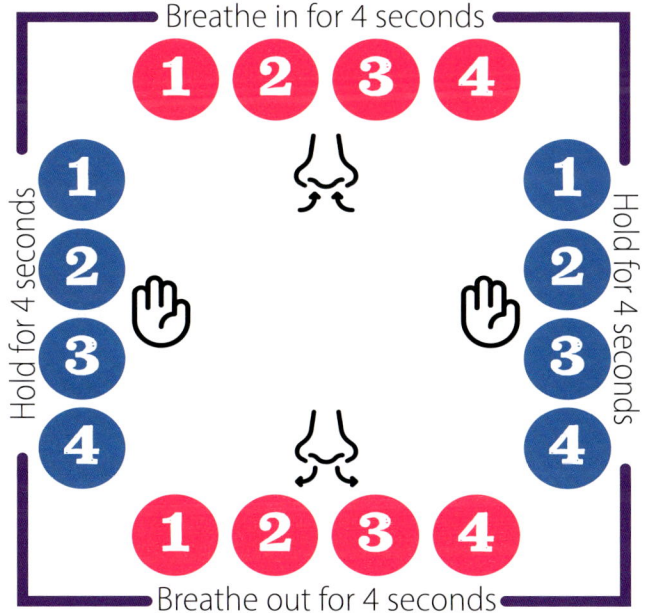

Some people also find it helpful to picture themselves in their favourite place whilst deep breathing. Try picturing yourself in your favourite place and think about what you can see, smell and feel.

### Go for a walk

Going for a walk after school or work is a great way to unwind and reflect on your day, leaving you feeling refreshed.

### Take time away from screens

With phone alerts and notifications going off all day long it can be difficult to wind down. Why not take some time away from your phone to read a book, listen to music or practise a breathing exercise? Learn more about the effects of screentime on our health.

### Mindfulness

Being 'mindful' just means being aware of everything around you in the present moment. It can help to put thoughts into perspective and gives you a break from the stress of worrying about past or future events. This should help you to feel more relaxed throughout the day.

It's about being aware of your surroundings and accepting them in a non-judgmental and welcoming way. Mindfulness might be more difficult to start with, and that's okay. Just like with anything else, practice makes perfect, and each person will find that different things help them to be mindful of their surroundings.

*9 June 2022*

---

### Design

Design a poster aimed at encouraging young people to cut down on screen time and spend more time outdoors. Highlight the benefits this would have to their mental health. Where would you display this poster?

The above information is reprinted with kind permission from Health For Teens.
© 2023 NHS

www.healthforteens.co.uk

# Group course can be standard treatment for anxiety and depression, trial finds

The first ever trial of a revolutionary group approach to anxiety and depression has shown it is no less effective than the one on one sessions thousands of people receive on the NHS every day.

The trial compared the 'Take Control Course' for up to 20 people – devised by researchers at the University of Manchester – with standard talking therapy. Both took place in six weekly sessions.

The study is published in the journal Cognitive Behavioural Therapy and funded by the Economic and Social Research Council.

The course – based on Perceptual Control Theory- follows a precise programme, teaching attendees about the importance of control in life – when to pursue it, when to let go and how to balance conflicting priorities.

They learn how to face long-standing fears and anxieties, and how to see the bigger picture and longer term goals, drawing on their own strengths.

Participants aren't required to talk about their mental health, but can if they wish.

The randomised controlled trial, conducted by The University of Manchester-led-team involved 156 people who were recruited from the NHS Improving Access to Psychological Therapies (IAPT) service.

They were offered either the Take Control Course or the established six sessions of one-to- one therapy provided by IAPT.

Participants, mostly referred by their GP, were recruited from Salford Six Degrees Social Enterprise, a low-intensity IAPT Service.

After a six month follow up, there was no evidence of a difference in mental health outcomes between the two interventions. After another six months, however, there was not enough data to give conclusive results.

The measures used by the researchers included a Patient Health Questionnaire Depression Scale, Generalised Anxiety Disorder Questionnaire as well as other psychological tools.

Though the course has been delivered by Six Degrees over the past eight years and has been adapted for use in high schools for the Manchester Healthy Schools, this is the first time it has been assessed by a randomised trial. It has also been delivered online.

Lydia Morris, Clinical Lecturer at University of Manchester, was the lead author, working with Warren Mansell, Honorary Reader at The University of Manchester and Professor of Mental Health at Curtin University, Perth.

He said: 'There are many effective talking therapies for common mental health problems such as anxiety and depression.

'However, training therapists are expensive, and some people prefer to meet in groups, rather than to talking to someone about their problems.

'The success of one-to-one talking therapies may often depend on the match between the therapist and client.

'The Take Control course, however is always delivered in exactly the same format.' Dr Morris co-developed the course as part of her PhD research.

She said: 'This trial showed the Take Control Course could be an efficient alternative to one-to-one therapy for common mental health problems, as well as providing an evidence-based alternative for people who do not want individual therapy.'

Co-author Tanya Wallwork has been working with Salford Six Degrees over the past decade and was a co-author of the manual used by facilitators of the course:

She said: 'As soon as I came across this course I knew how useful it could be. And the outcomes bear that out. Each week we use objective measures to assess the impact of using taking part in the course and the results are consistently good.

'The course came into its own during Covid when we started to give it via Zoom. It actually gives participants more choice- as they can choose to be visible or not.'

One participant in the course said: 'I found looking at goals and working out what's important to me really helpful. Especially when I think something I worry about too much is just a small thing but using the upward arrow technique to work out why it's important really helped me to look at the bigger picture rather than focusing on little things.'

The six sessions include:

- Discussing how life is about control – working out what we want to have more control of, and what we can have less control of.
- What Blocks Our Control? Even worry, rumination and self-criticism are a problem only to the extent they get in the way of important life goals.
- Feeling in Control Short-Term versus Getting Control of Your Life. Goals are organized hierarchically
- Taking Control of the Things Around You. A flexible way to work out what we have in common with people despite our disagreements
- Building on Strengths, Qualities, and Resources. Encourage participants to recall the strengths, qualities and resources they have, especially at times when things are difficult for them
- Moving Forward: What Gets Me Stuck? What Helps? Participants complete a worksheet on the things that are helping them feel in control and signs that they are struggling, like a 'relapse prevention' session in traditional CBT

*12 January 2023*

> 'This trial showed the Take Control Course could be an efficient alternative to one-to-one therapy for common mental health problems, as well as providing an evidence-based alternative for people who do not want individual therapy.'
>
> – Dr Lydia Morris

The above information is reprinted with kind permission from The University of Manchester
© 2023 The University of Manchester, all rights reserved

www.manchester.ac.uk

# Young people to be prescribed surfing and dancing by NHS to help anxiety

Study to assess if 'social prescribing' such as surfing or rollerskating can stop conditions worsening while on waiting lists.

By Denis Campbell, Health policy editor

Young people will take part in surfing, rollerskating and gardening to see whether sport, the arts and outdoor activities can make them less anxious and depressed.

NHS mental health trusts will use the activities to help 600 young people on their waiting lists for care as part of a study into whether 'social prescribing' helps improve mental wellbeing.

People aged 11 to 18 in 10 parts of England will also be able to take part in dance, music, sport and exercise and attend youth clubs during the trial, which is being run by academics from University College London.

If participation proves successful the NHS may seek to make such activities available across England as a way of helping the many thousands of young people who face what can be months-long delays in accessing formal treatment, during which time their condition often worsens.

'Young people's mental health is one of the greatest challenges facing the NHS,' said Dr Daisy Fancourt, the UCL mental health expert running the trial. 'Currently many young people referred to child and adolescent mental health services face long waits, during which time more than three-quarters experience a deterioration in their mental health.

'Social prescribing has the potential to support young people while they wait, by providing access to a range of creative and social activities that could enhance their confidence, self-esteem and social support networks.'

Fancourt and her team will assess how much young people participate, the feasibility of making such activities available and the costs involved. Participants will be able to choose which pursuits they want to try, aided by a link worker or 'buddy', in conjunction with 10 NHS mental health trusts.

This approach has been tested before in a small-scale trial conducted in Luton, Sheffield and Brighton & Hove in 2018-2020 but the UCL-led study will be the largest yet.

The government-funded assessment of that pilot found involvement improved young people's personal and mental wellbeing, especially among those who were feeling the worst at the outset, and reduced loneliness.

Participants said: 'Link workers contributed to improving their sense of autonomy, reduced their sense of stigma around mental health challenges and filled a gap in mental health service provision by providing almost immediate access to non-clinically based emotional support.' However, transport to and the cost of some activities proved problematic.

GPs are increasingly using 'social prescribing' – including gardening, bingo sessions and dance classes – as an alternative to antidepressants for adult patients who are lonely or depressed. However, recent research published in the medical journal BMJ Open raised serious doubts about its effectiveness.

But Fancourt insisted social prescribing had 'enormous potential' and could 'help address determinants of mental illness, decrease stigma and shame sometimes associated with mental health problems, and give young people choice and control of their care'.

The World Health Organization advocates physical activities, especially outdoors, as an aid to both physical and mental health.

'Social prescribing – involving activities like exercise, gardening and music – is a really exciting way of improving mental wellbeing. It looks at people holistically and tries to find non-medicalised ways of helping them find a way through the challenges they may be experiencing,' said Olly Parker, the head of external affairs at the charity YoungMinds.

'However, it cannot be a substitute for other types of support such as talking therapies.'

He added: 'Previous studies of social prescribing have yielded positive results with participants reporting increased levels of wellbeing and we're happy that further work is being done to see what further benefits there are for children and young people from this approach.'

The UCL trial is being funded by the Prudence Trust, a grant-making charity that focuses on young people's mental health services.

*25 October 2022*

### Key Fact

- GPs are increasingly using 'social prescribing' as an alternative to antidepressants for adult patients who are lonely or depressed.

The above information is reprinted with kind permission from *The Guardian*.
© 2023 Guardian News and Media Limited

www.theguardian.com

# A personal reflection: the drugs do work – taking SSRIs for panic disorder

By Ruth Cooper-Dickson – No Panic Patron

The journey of recovery from mental ill health can be tough to navigate. It isn't as straightforward as a broken arm or a chest infection, where diagnosis and treatment plan is clear. It's not linear and everyone is unique.

Medication is still a treatment which has stigma attached to it. A ground-breaking study published earlier this year demonstrated that antidepressants are effective and in fact more patients should be getting the right support through medication. Doctors hoped the study would finally put rest to doubts about the medicine, breaking the frequently portrayed stigma. For example, 'happy pills' is a phrase often used by the tabloids to describe the medication. This serves only to compound the opinion that an individual taking antidepressants such as SSRIs (selective serotonin reuptake inhibitors) is miserable, weak and unable to be happy in life.

Three years ago I had a severe panic attack and breakdown. At my first appointment my GP asked me if I wanted to take medication with no real explanation. It was like being asked if I would like to take insulin for diabetes. How would I know!? I wasn't the expert! My immediate reaction was 'no'! The stereotype in my head was of a numb, unfeeling individual and I didn't want people to think I was crazy. I didn't want to think I was crazy! Instead I opted for counselling and a mixture of talking therapies and Cognitive Behavioural Therapy. I was diagnosed with Generalised Anxiety Disorder and Panic Disorder.

I'm a huge advocate for positive psychology – a new field of research – and I have spent the last three years building up strong foundations of practice. This includes mindfulness meditation, yoga, exercise, gratitude, journaling and a growing bibliotherapy. Yet the deterioration of my mental wellbeing in July last year made it clear to me that I needed to go back to my GP.

This time my GP was amazing and talked me through everything. I had made my appointment a month in advance and decided I would go if I still thought it was a necessity. She was pleased that I had come to see her feeling well rather than in the depths of anxiety. Often people cancel their appointments for depression or anxiety because they don't want to bother their GP. It feels trivial or they start to feel better in themselves, a pattern I had seen emerging over a period of time. This time, I was able to have a rational

conversation about how the past nine months had affected me. The doctor agreed my lifestyle practices were well-versed; I had CBT exercises in my toolbox, so medication was the next route.

Throughout the first week of taking the tablets I had awful physical side-effects. Within an hour of taking my tablet in the morning I would feel nauseous and for the rest of the day I'd feel weak. I couldn't enjoy food, it kept going round and round in my mouth. My mouth was dry. My energy levels were low from my lack of appetite and food intake. A psychologist I connected with through Instagram saw my posts about struggling with the tablets. She contacted me and advised me to try taking them in the evening. Within four days I was feeling much better. Taking the tablet before I went to sleep allowed the nausea to disappear and didn't affect my sleep. I still have the dry mouth, which means I drink more – especially when presenting. This also means more frequent trips to the bathroom!

Taking my medication was a learning curve. It will affect each person differently. For me, I find alcohol does not agree with the medication at all. Even if I have one or two glasses of wine of a night, I can tell the difference the next day. I drink black coffee, but I have cut back after experiencing the start of a panic attack after drinking two strong Americanos. Mentally I have been feeling good. Some people experience heightened anxious feelings when they start taking the medication, a side-effect I managed to avoid.

I've tried to be open and challenge the conversation around the stigma of taking medication, even when it has made me feel uncomfortable. When I met with a potential new client who was recovering from visible surgery, we spoke about her operation and rehabilitation. When she enquired how I was, I replied that I was feeling nauseous as I had started taking SSRIs. This turned into an open conversation about her own personal experience. She has since booked me as a speaker for her employee network group.

I'm due back at the GP next week to review my progress. The medication has settled and I've noticed I am much better in myself. There have been several times I realised the physical symptoms I usually experience with my anxiety have not happened. My brain is not triggering any warning signs. I've been keeping a mood journal for the past two months and my moods are balanced. My family have noticed the lack of swinging between extreme emotions. As far as my recovery goes I am not sure how long I will take the medication. But if it means continuing to take them and being able to live my most best life, then that is part of my own journey.

I'd like to share my own tips based on my experience.

- Keep your doctor's appointment, even if you begin to feel better. It helped me to write everything down

beforehand so I was clear about what I wanted to discuss. If you need moral support take someone with you to the appointment to wait for you.

- Ensure you take in all the information from your GP. Ask if you or they can write this down in your appointment, or ask them to signpost you to further information.

- Be as open and honest with your manager or colleagues as possible. The side effects of medication can affect you physically and/or mentally in the first few weeks before settling, so it will definitely help to have the right support.

- Be kind to yourself whilst the medication settles. This could mean a change in your appetite, energy levels or mood. It will pass and if the symptoms persist or if you have concerns, make an appointment to see your doctor straightaway.

- If you do need to talk to someone for professional support you can call and speak to someone for anxiety at No Panic who have a crisis helpline 0300 7729844, or contact the Samaritans who are available 24 hours a day to provide confidential emotional support (116 123).

*29 October 2021*

The above information is reprinted with kind permission from No Panic.
© 2023 No Panic

www.nopanic.org.uk

# How therapy has helped me begin to tackle anxiety and overthinking

By NCS Writers' Club member Yasmin

Mental health and well-being is one of the biggest factors of a person's quality of life. It is being increasingly discussed throughout society, especially by younger generations who are taking more action and accountability over their wellbeing and going to therapy. There are many free NHS mental health and therapy services to utilise, as well as multiple private practices around the UK. To register for NHS therapy you can visit the UK Gov website and refer yourself through their online service, or you can book an appointment with your GP and they can refer you accordingly. To register for NHS therapy you must be registered at a UK GP practice.

Over the last few years I have been trialling different styles of therapy and different therapists to find the ones best-suited for me. Although there were a few bumps in the road, I've definitely gained a lot from all my experiences with therapy, and I would like to share some of the most important things I've learnt throughout my path to become the person I am, and who I continue to become. Please keep in mind that I am not a therapist or have any professional background to give advice from, this is purely from my own experience and how I have chosen to approach myself through therapy.

I struggle daily with anxiety and overthinking; I have always felt very trapped and stuck inside my mind, and I still do. However, I have begun to gain better skills in self-observation, which led me to be able to understand more about why I feel trapped, and start working through those mental blocks to further free myself from my limiting beliefs. One of the most effective ways I have managed to learn this is through the process of therapy itself. Hearing what my therapist has to say after I explain how I feel, and remembering that during troubling times, really helps me to hear a logical voice in my mind which isn't connected to my life through a personal relationship. To have someone who can healthily guide me to challenge my own inner dialogue and beliefs in a safe space has increased my ability to do it myself when I notice myself getting sucked into my thoughts.

You don't need to be mentally ill or have any severe mental issues to go to therapy. It is a brilliant method of gaining more emotional intelligence, depth, understanding of the self, and gives you skills to better cope with life's trials and tribulations when faced with them. I like thinking about therapy as a method of self-care, because it has greatly changed and impacted my life in multiple ways, and continues to do so profoundly.

I started journaling to do this, as it acts as an extension of my therapy sessions into something more tangible and creative, especially as a visual and artistic person. I treat my journal as a space of neutrality, honesty and truth, compassion, introspection, understanding, growth, and a place to dismantle my thoughts. It is somewhere I can write down everything that comes to mind without judgement. I can draw out my thoughts and feelings, study them with compassion, and pick out things that sound subjective and anchored to my own perspective in order to delve deeper and challenge those inner perceptions. Through journaling, I've given myself skills to guide similar trails of thought inside my mind without writing them down; this is helpful if I find myself overwhelmed in a situation where I cannot sit down to journal. I do this through meditation, which is another practice that has helped me significantly on multiple occasions, and continues to improve my wellbeing especially in the way in which I utilise it.

I give myself some time to breathe deeply into my body, and remind myself that the body and mind are always able to balance each other to a great degree when either one is out of alignment. When my mind is off course, I can use my physical body to gain back some of that stability and calmness. And when my body experiences physical symptoms of anxiety and instability, I can use my mind to step back and prevent myself from defining those experiences as truths about who I am in that moment, or feeling completely lost and overwhelmed by my feelings. It has taken a long time for me to be able to observe myself and attach myself less to my thoughts and feelings. I believe that starting small helps build that consistency and confidence to do so when trying to tackle larger-scale things.

A significant thing that has allowed me to do this is simply allowing myself to feel and think whatever I do without labelling it as good or bad, or right or wrong. Everything we feel and think is a reflection of our perspective of our lives. This can be used as a powerful telescope into past experiences and emotions which are unhealed, which cause us to react in the ways we do in the present moment. Understanding this and looking at yourself with a lens of neutrality is so important, because you begin creating that same non-judgemental space within yourself in order to feel safer in your own body. You can allow yourself to experience every emotion and thought without categorising or compartmentalising it as a way to make sense of it straight away. Everything you experience can be seen as a message; your mind and body are simply reacting. The ways in which you interpret those reactions determines how much you're able to understand and learn about yourself and what you are experiencing.

If you find yourself overwhelmed but cannot word the emotions you feel or why you are feeling them, you can begin by validating the physical experiences you're having.

Such as, 'I feel a tightness in my stomach. My breath is shallow. My heart is pounding'. Then, you can create your own counter-affirmations to help soothe yourself according to the physical symptoms you're experiencing. Such as, 'I am safe. I can experience symptoms of anxiety and still be safe and loved. I am experiencing difficult physical symptoms and that is okay. I am still me, worthy, and valuable, even whilst experiencing anxiety. I allow myself to experience the present moment with no judgement. It is okay to allow my body to express itself in this manner. These symptoms are temporary, and I will soon find calmness once again'.

Doing this whenever you notice yourself having a reaction, minuscule or not, helps guide your way of thinking into one of compassion, instead of judging yourself and criticising yourself. Once you have practiced this method of just allowing yourself to 'be' and 'experience' without judgement, you can begin to ask yourself questions to deepen your understanding of why you experienced something difficult or uncomfortable within yourself. You can use these questions as journal prompts or things you can think about. Some questions can be, 'What about -said situation- made me the most uncomfortable? Have I experienced this emotion/reaction before? If so, when was it? What happened? Did I feel that my emotions were validated and understood? Am I reacting to this past situation in my present moment? Am I giving the present moment a narrative/story from my past in order to express what I wish I had said/done? Am I reacting appropriately to the reality of the present moment or am I reacting out of fear of past pain and hurt? What can I do right now to validate my feelings and express myself in a healthy and safe way?'

There are many more questions like these you could ask depending on your individual situation, these are just a few which have helped me immensely when I'm trying to understand my own reactions and triggers to things. The real difficulty of these questions is being completely truthful and honest in every single answer. Sometimes it takes multiple times asking yourself these questions to get to the root of what has caused you to react, and more often than not there is always more than one cause/trauma which has built up to form these reactions. There is nothing wrong with experiencing triggers and responses to things, but it is our own responsibility to take accountability for our self-improvement and develop better coping skills in order to give ourselves a better quality of life, and in turn, give others the opportunity to have a better and healthier relationship with us.

I hope that this has given you some insight and ideas about how to begin tackling the more uncomfortable aspects of yourselves on a daily basis. Thank you for reading!

*18 January 2022*

### Think!

Think about times when you have felt anxious or depressed in the past. What did you do that helped you to process how you were feeling? Did you write a journal, talk to a friend, listen to particular music or maybe even get into gardening? As a class create a 'feel-good' list of activities that have helped lift your spirits when you needed it most.

The above information is reprinted with kind permission from National Citizen Service. © 2023 NCS

**www.wearencs.com**

# Three ways to tackle the 'Sunday scaries', the anxiety and dread many people feel at the end of the weekend

An article from The Conversation.

By Jolanta Burke, Senior Lecturer, Centre for Positive Psychology and Health, RCSI University of Medicine and Health Sciences

Sunday is often a chance to catch up with friends, lost sleep, and recover from last night's hangover. But for many of us, by the time Sunday afternoon rolls around, a feeling of intense anxiety and dread sets in – often referred to as the 'Sunday scaries'.

It's hardly surprising the 'Sunday scaries' are so common. After all, research shows Sunday is our unhappiest day of the week – with Saturday being the peak. There are a number of reasons why the Sunday scaries happen, and how you spend your weekend can play a big role.

For example, spending all your weekend stuck inside on your computer probably isn't a good idea, even if it's for leisure. This is because research shows people who spend a lot of time on their computer tend to feel more anxious in general. Abundant alcohol and drug use can also cause your mood to plummet and cause anxiety levels to soar the following day. So if you spent your Saturday night partying, this might explain why you feel down or anxious by Sunday afternoon.

For many people, the Sunday scaries also happen due to the work they left behind on Friday evening. The anticipation of the next day, the work you might have to do, and all the emails you'll need to catch up on can cause anxiety. But working through the weekend isn't the answer either – and could actually leave your mental health worse off.

The Sunday scaries may also happen because of a social overload that happens during the weekend. This may be especially true for people who work hard during the week or those who are single, who designate their weekend as being their primary time for socialising. But spending time with others, as enjoyable as it may be, can put additional pressure on us. For example, when we share our friends' worries, we may become stressed too..

If you're someone who tends to suffer from the Sunday scaries, here are a few things you can do to cope.

### 1. Finish your tasks

One of the most effective ways of getting rid of the Sunday scaries is to prevent them from happening to begin with. This means trying to finish any tasks you need to do before the weekend, instead of leaving it until Monday morning.

When you know you have unfinished business to deal with on Monday, it can have a number of effects on you, including by ruining your night's sleep and making you more anxious on Sunday. It may even affect your next week by making you more likely to experience burnout. This is why starting the week with a clean slate is crucial.

Before you switch off your computer on Friday evening, you might also want to take time to reflect on the negative things that may have happened during the week, consider what changes you might want to make for the next week, and try to tie up any loose ends and easy tasks that you can instead of leaving them for Monday.

If you're in a middle of a long-term project, at least try to complete a milestone task that will help you feel like a chapter of your work is closed on Friday, with a new one ready to begin on Monday.

### 2. Positive anticipation

Probably the biggest reason for feeling anxious on Sunday evening is due to dreading the work you have to do the following week – especially those tasks you hate doing.

But having events planned for the week that you can look forward to can help balance out these negative emotions and make you feel more positive about the week head. Try creating a new routine on Sunday where you plan out fun things you can do the next week, such as meeting friends for lunch or going to the cinema after work.

### 3. Write it down

If you get your Sunday scaries but have no idea what's causing them, take 20 minutes of uninterrupted time to write down your deepest thoughts and feelings. This simple exercise can help you figure out what causes your anxious thoughts, which will ultimately help you address them.

But if you're someone who has never tried expressive writing before, here are a few things that might help you get started:

- Write about your challenges using a different perspective (such as how your parent or best friend might see it).
- Try writing at different times of day. You may be more focused at different times of the day, which can be important for helping you tune into how you're feeling.
- If you find it difficult to talk or write about yourself, imagine you're writing with a specific audience in mind, such as your friend. This may help you better express what you're feeling and understand why you're feeling that way.

### Activity

Try to write down any anxious thoughts that you have. What are you concerned about? See if writing the thoughts down make them less scary.

- If writing isn't for you, use a recorder or video to help you express yourself.

Of course, there are many reasons that people may experience the Sunday scaries. While some of these factors we can change, some of them are a bit more difficult to address, such as if your feelings of anxiety are due to working with people who treat you unfairly.

But regardless of the reasons you may get the Sunday scaries, remember that we often tend to over-exaggerate our anxieties in our heads – and often these fears turn out to be unfounded.

*29 July 2022*

**THE CONVERSATION**

The above information is reprinted with kind permission from The Conversation.
© 2010-2023, The Conversation Trust (UK) Limited

www.theconversation.com

# How to use the 333 rule for anxiety

Feeling anxious? This simple trick can help alleviate some of those worries.

By Laura Hampson

At any one time, there are around eight million people in the UK experiencing some form of anxiety disorder.

This can range from a panic disorder, to social anxiety, to post-traumatic stress, and phobias such as claustrophobia or agoraphobia.

According to the NHS, while most people experience feelings of anxiety at one point or another, some find it harder to control their worries and feelings of anxiety have a more constant effect on their daily lives.

A 2014 study from YouGov found that one in five people who experience anxiety have no coping mechanisms to help them through it.

While the health service suggests treatments such as therapy or antidepressant medicines, there are other things you can do to help manage those feelings.

One of these methods is known as the '333 rule'. According to Healthline, the 333 rule is an informal technique for coping with anxiety.

It can help to keep you grounded and 'calm down in a moment where you are feeling particularly anxious or overwhelmed'.

The 333 rule consists of three factors. When you're feeling anxious, you'll need to look around your current environment and:

- Name three things you see
- Identify three sounds you hear
- Move three things, such as your arms or legs, or touch three things such as an object

A recent TikTok video posted by mental health membership club Mind Bar said: 'Practicing this method is an easy tool to bring you back to the present moment.'

While there have been no scientific studies into the effectiveness of the 333 rule, it can be a helpful aid to manage anxiety.

Other ways to help reduce feeling of anxiety, according to the NHS, include going on a self-help course, exercising regularly, stopping smoking, and cutting down on the amount of alcohol you consume.

*5 December 2022*

The above information is reprinted with kind permission from The Independent.
© independent.co.uk 2023

www.independent.co.uk

# Further Reading/ Useful Websites

## Useful Websites

www.bps.org.uk

www.championhealth.co.uk

www.healthforteens.co.uk

www.independent.co.uk

www.inews.co.uk

www.manchester.ac.uk

www.mentalhealth.org.uk

www.mind.org.uk

www.nhs.uk

www.nopanic.org.uk

www.ox.ac.uk

www.shoutoutuk.org

www.telegraph.co.uk

www.theconversation.com

www.theguardian.com

www.wearencs.com

www.weforum.org

www.who.int

Page 7: read the full report: https://championhealth.co.uk/insights/guides/workplace-health-report/

Page 19: www.who.int/news/item/02-03-2022-covid-19-pandemic-triggers-25-increase-in-prevalence-of-anxiety-and-depression-worldwide

*Future Tense: Why Anxiety Is Good for You (Even Though it Feels Bad)*, by psychologist Tracy Dennis-Tiwar

*First Steps Out of Anxiety* by Dr Kate Middleton

*The Power of Regret* by Daniel Pink

*Bittersweet* by Susan Cain

## Where can I find help?

Below are some telephone numbers, email addresses and websites of agencies or charities that can offer support or advice if you, or someone you know needs it.

**Anxiety UK**
Helpline: 03444 775 774
www.anxietyuk.org.uk

**ChildLine**
Helpline: 0800 11 11
www.childline.org.uk

**Mind**
MindInfoline: 0300 123 3393
www.mind.org.uk

**No Panic**
Youth Line: 0330 606 1174
www.nopanic.org.uk

**YoungMinds**
Helpline: 0808 802 5544
www.youngminds.org.uk

# Glossary

### Angst
A feeling of anxiety or apprehension.

### Antidepressants
These include tricyclic antidepressants (TCAs), selective serotonin re-uptake inhibitors (SSRIs) and monoamine oxidase inhibitors (MAOIs). Antidepressants work by boosting one or more chemicals (neurotransmitters) in the nervous system, which may be present in insufficient amounts during a depressive illness.

### Anxiety
Feeling nervous, worried or distressed, sometimes to a point where the person feels so overwhelmed that they find everyday life very difficult to handle.

### Burnout
Burnout is most commonly spoken of in work-related terms. It occurs when things have gone out of balance, and our stress and activity levels far outweigh the amount of rest we have.

### Cognitive behavioural therapy (CBT)
A psychological treatment which assumes that behavioural and emotional reactions are learned over a long period. A cognitive therapist will seek to identify the source of emotional problems and develop techniques to overcome them.

### Counselling
Sometimes known as talk therapy, allows people to talk through their emotions and their decisions to hurt themselves. The counsellor or therapist provides support and may be able to teach self-harmers how to make more healthy choices in the future.

### Depression
Someone is said to be significantly depressed, or suffering from depression, when feelings of sadness or misery don't go away quickly and are so bad that they interfere with everyday life. Symptoms can also include low self-esteem and a lack of motivation. Depression can be triggered by a traumatic/difficult event (reactive depression), but not always (e.g. endogenous depression).

### Generalised anxiety disorder (GAD)
Someone with GAD has a lot of anxiety (feeling fearful, worried and tense) on most days, and not just in specific situations, and the condition persists long-term. Some of the physical symptoms of anxiety come and go. Someone with this high level of `background anxiety` may also have panic attacks and some phobias.

### Hidden disabilities
Not all disabilities are obvious. An individual who suffers from epilepsy, mental ill health or diabetes still faces the challenge of coping with a disability but is often not recognised as a disabled person, since to a casual observer they do not display the outward symptoms often associated with disability.

### Intervention
The process of getting someone to seek professional help for the treatment of a disorder, condition or addiction.

### Mental health/well-being
Everyone has 'mental health'. It includes our emotional, psychological and social well-being. It affects how we think, feel, and act. It also helps determine how we handle stress, relate to others, and make choices. Mental health is important at every stage of life, from childhood and adolescence through adulthood.

### Mindfulness
Mind-body based training that uses meditation, breathing and yoga techniques to help you focus on your thoughts and feelings. Mindfulness helps you manage your thoughts and feelings better, instead of being overwhelmed by them.

### Panic attack
A panic attack is a severe attack of anxiety and fear which occurs suddenly, often without warning, and for no apparent reason. Symptoms can include palpitations, sweating, trembling, nausea and hyperventilation. At least one in ten people have occasional panic attacks. They tend to occur most in young adults.

### Social anxiety disorder
Fear of social situations.

### SSRIs
Selective serotonin reuptake inhibitors. A medication widely used to treat depression and anxiety.

### Stress
Stress is the feeling of being under pressure. A little bit of pressure can be a good thing, helping to motivate you: however, too much pressure or prolonged pressure can lead to stress, which is unhealthy for the mind and body and can cause symptoms such as lack of sleep, loss of appetite and difficulty concentrating.

### Talking therapies
These involve talking and listening. Some therapists will aim to find the root cause of a sufferer's problem and help them deal with it, some will help to change behaviour and negative thoughts, while others simply offer support.

# Index

**A**
alcohol 2
anger 12
anti-anxiety medication *see* medication
antidepressants 27, 43
   *see also* medication
anxiety
   causes of 2, 3, 13–14, 24–25
   purpose of 10–12
   as a side effect 2
   statistics 6–7
   symptoms 3
   treatments 26–28
   triggers 2, 15
applied relaxation 26
autism 5

**B**
benzodiazepines 28
blood sugar 24
body image 22
brain studies 13–14
breathing exercises 31
burnout 40, 43

**C**
caffeine 24
causes of anxiety 2, 3, 13–14, 24–25
childhood experiences 2
climate anxiety 17–20
cognitive behavioural therapy (CBT) 11, 26, 36, 43
counselling 43
   *see also* talking therapies
COVID-19 pandemic, impact of 1, 8, 15–16, 19

**D**
depression 6–9, 13–14, 43
diet, and anxiety 2, 24–25
dopamine 11

**E**
eco-anxiety 17–20
emotions, purpose of 10–12
employee anxiety 6–7
existential anxiety 25

**F**
fear 10–11
finances 21
frontal lobe 13–14

**G**
generalised anxiety disorder (GAD) 26–28, 36–37, 43
Good Childhood Report 2021 1
group therapy 32–33

**H**
heart disease 14
hidden disabilities 43

**I**
immune system 11
intervention 5, 32, 43

**J**
journaling 38–39, 41

**L**
language, and mental health 1, 4
lockdown *see* COVID-19 pandemic
loneliness 15

**M**
medication 11, 24, 26–28, 36–37
mental health, definition 43
mindfulness 31, 43

**P**
panic attacks 2, 3, 36–37, 43
phone call anxiety 23
physical health, and anxiety 2, 24–25
practical anxiety 17
pregabalin 27–28
PTSD (post-traumatic stress disorder) 19

**R**
regret 12
relaxation 26, 31

**S**
sadness 12
selective serotonin reuptake inhibitor (SSRI) 27, 36–37
sensory hyper-reactivity 5
separation anxiety 2
serotonin and noradrenaline reuptake inhibitors (SNRIs) 27
social anxiety disorder 5, 23, 43
social isolation 15
social prescribing 34–35
stigma 36
stress 6, 43
subgenual anterior cingulate cortex (sgACC) 13–14
suicidal thinking 15

Sunday scaries 40–41
support, sources of 30
   *see also* treatments
symptoms 3

**T**
talking therapies 7, 23, 26, 32–33, 36, 38–39, 43
treatments 26–28, 31–41
triggers 2, 15

**W**
weather, extreme 19
   *see also* climate anxiety
women and girls, and anxiety 22
Workplace Health Report 6–7
world events 29

**Y**
Young Lives project 8–9